Saddler & Scout

Nicole Rodrigues

Saddler
Series

Book 1

#rideamustacke

Printed in the United States of America.

First Printing, 2019. Independently Published.

ISBN 9781097995691

@nicolerodriguesauthor

Table of Contents

Acknowledgments

First and foremost, I wanted to thank my husband. My best friend, my supporter, my cover model. This dream wouldn't be possible without you by my side. Thank you for always keeping me on my toes and making me push myself to become better. Your filthy mouth and hilarious comebacks are what makes these books so enjoyable, so thanks for being such a perv and inspiring them <3

Thank you to my "Saddler Squad"! My hype women that I would not be able to do this without! You all make this so much more fun for me and your support is everything! I appreciate all the shares, the kind words, the amazing pictures and everything else and in between.

My bookwife, Emina and bookbestie, Britney for keeping me sane when I feel anything but. For telling me when my teasers are crap and sending me endless funny gifs and videos to keep me from throwing my laptop out my window.

My BBB's! The support of authors in this community is overwhelming and these ladies have my heart! I always feel loved and know that at the end of the day, I have found my tribe of amazing, kickass women!

Last, but certainly not least, you readers! Thank you for taking this journey with me! If there was no you, there would be no me! Thanks for enjoying the words I pour out on these pages! You give me life!

Saddler's Secret

Machlin Saddler

Uber asshole, real estate mogul, sexy as hell and CEO of
Saddler Enterprises, where I now work. Heartbreaking
circumstances thrusts me into motherhood, and on the
plane ride home, I break down, kissing a total stranger and
the angel offered me a solution; Saddler Enterprises. I've
climbed the ladder and worked my ass off for months, and
in walks, Adam, our intern. I try to keep things professional
but all of a sudden, I start to find him funny and charming.
His kiss electrifies me but that's precisely when shit really
hits the fan.

Suddenly, I'm on the mysterious Machlin Saddler's radar.
Big, bad CEO that never makes his way to our floor, now
makes it his new stomping grounds. He lights my body on
fire like no one has before. He's alluring and gorgeous and
I'm being pulled in two different directions. Only the new
intern isn't who I think he is. He's the perfect stranger from
the plane I took to start my new life with Kenzie. The
perfect stranger I kissed. The perfect stranger I hate.

Genevieve Langston

The breathtaking woman I haven't been able to keep my
mind off of, has been my downfall. I need her like a lion
needs prey but I can't screw up the plan. She'll hate me, hell
she already does, but the line between love and hate is very,
very thin.

"Unless it's mad, passionate, extraordinary love, it's a waste of your time. There are too many mediocre things in life. Love shouldn't be one of them."

— Dreams for an Insomniac

Prologue
Genevieve

I adjust Kenzie on my hip, the backpack on my shoulder slipping off again as I stand in the waiting area to board the plane to Arizona--to home--or whatever is left of it.

My father died ten years ago, I was the only child and my mother is a shell of the woman she once was. I'm desperate though, nowhere else to go as Kenzie fusses, burying her face in my chest.

She's had a rough week, hell I've had a rough week too and I just want to curl up in bed and cry, but I can't. I need to be strong for her. *Tonya* needs me to be strong for Kenzie.

She fusses again, a little louder this time and I see people's heads start to turn.

"It's okay, baby, almost our turn, okay? Look at the big airplane," I coax, walking towards the window, pointing.

She slams her hand on the glass, laughing and then leans forward, banging her head against it, letting out a loud wail.

"Shit," I grumble. "It's okay, baby. It's okay," I soothe.

I kneel, dropping the bag from my shoulder and hold her to my chest tightly as I hear our row being called to board.

I grab the backpack from the floor with a crying Kenzie and walk to the front, handing our tickets to the attendant. She gives me a sympathetic smile, glancing down at my hand briefly before handing me back our tickets.

No ring, bring on the pity face.

I walk down the aisle to our seats and thank the Lord when I see that it's a window and middle. Although I'm not sure Kenzie can survive another headbutt with the glass, at least looking out the window will distract her.

She's calmed down now, playing with the window shade when something hard brushes against the back of my arm. I surmise it's the person sharing the row with us and move closer to Kenzie, giving the person some room. That's when I smell it: sensuality and elegance, strong yet subtle, crisp and fresh.

"Sorry about that, just putting my bag in the overhead compartment," says a deep, raspy voice.

My body shivers and I slowly turn to see the sexiest, most rugged man I've ever laid eyes on. His unruly brown hair is long and curly past his ears, his beard is groomed to perfection down to his chest and his eyes, a dark chocolate brown that sparkle with a smile. He's so handsome, I almost forget to breathe, let alone nod as an answer.

"I double checked my ticket and this is my seat. I wasn't sure if your husband was--"

"No husband," I interrupt. "It's all yours."

He gives me a smile and my heart that's been shattered this past week, jump starts to life and flutters. *Tonya, you sneaky, sneaky woman.*

I smile and laugh, thinking about Tonya watching down over Kenzie and me, planting this enigma of a man right here next to us on the plane. I imagine calling and telling her about the encounter and her laughing, telling me I should have gone for it; asked him out and taken life by the horns like she would have.

I don't realize when my laugh has turned into a cry but I'm holding Kenzie, both of us crying as the stranger puts his strong hand on my back, his look of pity and concern makes me cry harder.

"I'm...s-so...s-sorry," I stutter through the tears. "M-my best friend just...d-died and I have her b-baby and I'm t-trying to k-keep everything t-together."

Over the speakers, the pilot tells us to get buckled as I strap Kenzie next to me, wiping my tears of sadness and embarrassment. Kenzie starts crying harder now as we take off and I don't know how to calm her.

Tonya and I lived together but whenever Kenzie had a meltdown, Tonya knew what to do. I'm not even sure she did anything, she was just *mom*. It was a feeling of safety Kenzie felt--of pure motherly love. I'm not her mom; I'm just fun Auntie Genn. I can barely take care of myself, let alone her. It was in the will Tonya had drawn up when Kenzie was born, though. She had no family, and Kenzie's dad was a piece of shit that bailed before the pee even dried on the pregnancy test. It's been the three of us for so long, but now, it's just the two of us.

I try to soothe her as best as I possibly can, but she just keeps crying and I'm grateful for the seatbelt sign being lifted. I unbuckle her, bringing her to my lap but she keeps crying. I feel everyone on the plane staring at us and I glance over at the man sharing our row.

"I'm so sorry about this."

I hold back the tears, unsure of what to do and the man smiles.

"Don't apologize. May I?" asks the handsome stranger.

He motions for Kenzie and I nod, passing her over to him. First day of parenthood and I'm officially failing, handing my kid to a stranger.

The man reaches inside his flannel jacket for a lollipop and Kenzie's eyes light up, her crying slowly subsiding.

He unwraps the lollipop and eyes me, questioning if he could give it to her.

"Probably should have asked before you took it out of your pocket, no?" I laugh, wiping my tears.

He smiles sheepishly and drops his head.

"Probably, I'm sorry. I didn't mean to overstep."

"It's okay, she can have it."

"Here ya go, cutie."

Kenzie takes the lollipop and drops her head to the man's chest with a smile.

"How did you do that? I mean I get the candy, but..."

"Younger sisters and I happen to know how painful it is to have your ears pop on planes. I had tubes put in my ears when I was younger. My parents always had to have a stash of lollipops whenever we traveled. It's the same for babies. I have extras for when we land, it'll happen again."

I open my mouth and then close it, amazed at the kindness of this stranger, literally sent from above.

"Thank you," I smile. "I can take her back. I didn't mean to hijack your whole flight."

"It's okay, she's fine. I'm MJ by the way," he says, extending his hand.

"Genevieve, and this is Mackenzie."

"So, what's bringing you to Arizona?"

"I uh...my mother is still there. Trying to figure out my next move. I couldn't...I couldn't stay in New York after losing my friend. Too many memories," I say, shaking my head, playing with the laces on Kenzie's shoe.

I look up and smile. Her head is against MJ's chest and the lollipop hangs out of her mouth, her eyes closed.

"I might have to take you home with me," I laugh, looking up at him.

His eyes darken and my smile fades.

"I...sorry that sounded...I meant...I..."

"I understood you," he says, amusement in his voice.

I clear my throat and shift a little in my seat.

"So, why are *you* traveling to Arizona?"

"It's home. Coming back from a business trip."

"That's exciting. What do you do?"

He looks like a blue-collar guy; flannel jacket, dark Wranglers and tan Timberland boots. Maybe he's a lumberjack.

"I'm in real estate."

"No frigging way! I have my real estate license! I mean I haven't done anything with it, truthfully. I've just been a secretary for a real estate company."

"Really? What were your responsibilities?" he asks, turning towards me.

"At first, getting my boss coffee and trying to avoid his grabby hands," I say, shaking my head.

MJ's jaw twitches and I clear my throat.

"I uh...he was fired for sexual harassment. Apparently, I wasn't the only one and we all spoke up. My new boss was amazing. She taught me a lot. I organized showings, helped stage, worked a little on the marketing side. Kind of a little bit of everything."

"It sounds like you knew what you were doing."

"Well, real estate in New York is tough. It's so competitive, so I really stayed in the background, never allowed on my own. I wasn't good enough to venture out, but one day," I say, giving him a small smile.

I remember briefly Tonya's last words to me before she left the apartment and never came back.

"I just want to sell! It's so frustrating being on the sidelines when you know you'll be a great asset to the team, ya know?" I groaned.

"When I get back from work tomorrow morning, you and I are gonna get some breakfast and work up a plan. The world needs you selling them houses, Genevieve Langston. You could sell a finished, furnished house to a God damn carpenter. He'll be standing in the middle of that brand-new house with all his tools scratching his head, wondering how the fuck it just happened. You'll be strutting your way to the bank and cash that 6% check like the boss bitch you are," Tonya said.

I wipe my eyes remembering the police officer at our door later that night, telling me she died at the scene of the accident on her way to the hospital for her night shift. A wrong way driver. I slept in her bed that night with Kenzie, crying into her pillow that smelt like her.

"Hey, it's okay," MJ soothes, pulling me closer to him.

I nod wiping my nose with my sweatshirt sleeve and lay my head on his shoulder. God, this man is a saint. I swear I'm going to leave this plane and look over to the aisle seat and it'll be empty. There is no way this man is real, this has to be a dream.

I feel a soft touch on my shoulder and open my eyes, getting my bearings.

"Hey, I didn't want to wake you, but I think we're gonna land soon," MJ whispers.

"Oh my gosh, I'm so sorry. I didn't mean to fall asleep..."

"It's okay. I figured you've had a restless week. I didn't mind."

I nod sitting up straighter and embarrassingly wipe the drool off the corner of my mouth. Kenzie is still sleeping in his lap and I smile.

"Let me ask you; where in Arizona are you staying?"

"My mother lives in Marana," I answer.

"Do you believe in fate, Genevieve?" MJ asks smiling.

"I...I didn't until today," I say softly.

"There's an opening at the company I work for and I think you would be a great fit. We're based in the city, so it would maybe be a twenty-minute drive for you. How about you take my card and come to the office on Monday. If you need to bring Kenzie, that's okay. We have an onsite childcare center."

"I...are you serious right now? I really want to pinch myself truthfully, this doesn't feel real," I laugh.

The pilot tells us to buckle up and prepare for landing as MJ buckles Kenzie into the seat with him. She's still catching flies as the flight attendant comes over to tell him Kenzie needs her own seat.

"Can you please get us the seat belt attachment. I'd rather not wake her, she's under the weight limit."

His voice is authoritative and the attendant nods, scurrying away and coming back with a seat belt attachment.

MJ pulls it through his seat belt and straps it around Kenzie.

He leans his head back and takes a lollipop out of his jacket.

"Dum dum?" he asks, while turning it towards me.

I smile and take it.

"Thank you."

He takes another lollipop out of his jacket and takes the wrapper off. I watch as he slips it inside his mouth, licking his lips.

My body is confused; one minute crying over Tonya and the next lusting over the distraction she clearly sent me from heaven. I wrack my brain for the last time that I had sex and can't even remember.

That guy from the gym? We went on a few dates and tried the whole sex thing. It was terrible; so terrible that I had to change gyms. When you have to ask the woman you're inside of if she orgasmed, you're not doing it right. That was months ago, and it really shouldn't even count.

"Genevieve?"

"Hmm?" I shake my head, snapping my attention back to MJ.

"I said, do you have a ride to your mother's? I can give you a lift?" he asks, standing in the aisle holding Kenzie.

When the hell did we even land?

"I...I don't...I mean, thank you, but I don't really know you," I say, finally realizing as perfect as this man is, he's still a stranger.

Too perfect. Wasn't there a serial killer that lured women in by his charm and good looks? No thanks.

"Fair enough," he smiles. "I'll help you get your luggage at least. I only have a carry on."

"Okay, thank you."

MJ reaches for my backpack in the overhead compartment, holding it and his own and a sleepy Kenzie.

He's tall, maybe 6'2, 6'3 with a fit body, like a swimmer. His jeans hug him like they're custom made and he effortlessly walks down the aisle of the plane as if he's not holding two bags and a three-year-old child.

He nods to the flight attendants and they both eye his ass appreciatively as he walks past. *I don't blame you ladies, not one bit.* He turns to wait for me to catch up and smirks when he catches me staring at his ass.

"The pickup is usually downstairs. How many bags do you have?"

"Just two. I sold everything in our apartment and boxed and shipped some of Tonya's things and a couple toys for Kenzie."

He nods as we continue to walk towards the escalators and take them down. He hands me Kenzie and stands at the luggage wheel, his stance powerful and dominant.

"Just point it out and I'll grab it, okay?" he commands, turning around.

"Okay."

He smiles at me, a small smirk and my stomach flips. He's handsome, so frigging handsome.

The sound of the belt moving breaks our gaze and I see our luggage, the first two ones out of the gate. This day isn't real. I expected them to be the last, or maybe even lost after having a whole plane ride of pure perfection.

"Those two," I say pointing.

MJ grabs the two when they come around, lifting them as if they were empty and not struggling at all when I know for a fact that they barely made the weight limit. Maybe that's the catch; they're empty. That's the black cloud on this sunny day, someone screwed with our luggage.

"Hold on a second," I say, unzipping the top of my luggage.

The zipper slides down but then catches on something. I struggle to pull it down, but MJ motions for me to step aside, sticking his fingers in the luggage while jiggling the zipper.

My cheeks heat when he pulls my black, lacey thong out of my luggage and the zipper slides down.

"These were in the way," he says with a grin.

"I..." my throat is dry as he chuckles, and I snatch my panties and shove them back in the luggage. "I just wanted to make sure that my clothes were actually in there."

"Why wouldn't they be?"

"You just...you lifted them too easily," I grumble.

He laughs again and nods for me to walk ahead of him to the exit.

"Are you sure I can't give you a ride? It really wouldn't be a problem. I promise I'm not a criminal."

"That sounds like something a criminal would say," I retort, arching my eyebrow.

"Fair enough. My treat though, okay?"

"MJ, I can't--"

"Let me. The first day of a new life. Let it start off on the right foot."

He reaches into his jacket pocket for a black business card with just a phone number, nothing else.

"Take this. Call it. Tell them MJ sent you and they'll explain the rest."

I take the card, wordlessly nodding as he pulls our luggage to the curb. He walks over to the man standing outside a sleek black car and the man nods, taking out his cell phone. I watch the exchange and after a few minutes, a taxi comes to the curb. MJ wheels our luggage to it, putting everything in the trunk and then walks around to the driver. He hands him a couple of bills and the driver takes it, bowing and thanking him over and over.

"All set. Need help strapping Kenzie? She should be in a car seat, no?" he asks, furrowing his brows.

"Oh my God! Yes, we checked it! I totally forgot!"

"I've got it. Hang here."

He walks back inside and emerges a couple of minutes later with Kenzie's car seat. He walks around to the other side, strapping it into the seat and nods for me to come around.

I put Kenzie in the car seat, making sure she is secure and then turn towards MJ, shutting the door.

"I...I don't know how to repay you for today. I...thank you so much. Your kindness was my saving grace."

He smiles and moves a piece of my hair off my forehead.

"It was my pleasure. Make sure you call that number. It was great to meet you, Genevieve."

I don't know what comes over me. Maybe Tonya temporarily invades my body to make sure I don't screw up the chance she has given me, but I cup MJ's cheek, pull him close to me and crash my lips against his. He stiffens against me but then relents, putting his hand on top of the taxi, lightly pushing my back against it. His hands go to my hips, his touch soft yet demanding as he tilts his head, devouring more of my mouth. I give it to him, I give it all to him but too soon he pulls away, both of us panting and our gazes confused. He felt it too, that explosion and he backs away slowly.

"Take care of yourself, Genevieve. Kenzie too. You'll be okay."

I nod and wave as he turns and gets into the sleek black car behind our taxi. I touch my lips as I mindlessly walk towards the other side of the car and get in. I haven't taken my fingers off my lips the entire ride to my mother's house.

What a man, what a kiss.

Machlin

I watch the taxi drive away and then tell my driver, Michael, to follow them. A woman and a child shouldn't travel alone; this is a sick fucking world.

I run my hand through my long, unruly hair and scratch my beard. Fuck, I can't wait to get cleaned up. I hate doing business overseas. My privacy is important to me though, so anytime I travel, I don't want to be recognized. My attire, my appearance, the way I travel is all...un-Machlin.

I reach up into my eyes, taking out my brown contacts and blink a couple of times. I grab my glasses out of my jacket and slide them on as I open my phone, checking my messages. I have one from my brother, Elijah, and dial his number, holding the phone to my ear as I scratch my jaw again.

"Mac, how did everything go?" Elijah asks.

"Great. They're on board with the Saddler Startup venture. I'll be back in a week or two to sort through everything. You do know who runs the offices over there, right?" I ask, amusement in my voice.

"I do and he's doing a great job."

"Rochelle isn't going to be happy if the board decides to send him over here, you know," I say, watching the taxi in front of us take the exit off the highway. "Fall back a little, I don't want her to get nervous that we're following," I inform my driver.

He nods and slows the car down, putting two more in between us and Genevive's taxi.

"Are you headed back to the office, or going on a heist?" Elijah asks with a laugh.

"I met a woman on the plane today, Genevieve Langston. I want you to look into her for me. She worked at a real estate company in New York. She's going to call the office for an interview. Don't mention my name, she got the card from an 'MJ'. If she checks out, give her a job. She did some side work by helping stage and secretarial stuff. I want to see what she can do."

"We're hiring strays now?"

"She's struggling, Elijah. Her best friend just died and left her with her daughter, a little girl that's maybe two or three. If she worked real estate in New York, we could use her with this Jeremy bullshit. She seems reliable."

"How can you tell that from one plane ride?" Elijah asks, incredulously.

He's right and I should be more wary, but I can't be. My pull to her, the feeling of comfort while sitting on the plane next to her, was addicting. I was just "MJ" not Machlin Saddler and it felt good, a brief break from the demands of my life; where everyone always needs something, the constant need to fix problems.

"It's just a feeling I get, okay? We can test her first, not throw her to the sharks right away. She could be the key though. We'll talk more when I get to the office. Is everything set up?"

"We're working out the details, you'll see when you get here. Are you sure you wanna do this?"

"I'm the only one that people rarely see, Elijah. It can't be you or Rochelle and I don't trust anyone else to do this," I say, watching the taxi pull into a driveway to a small, rundown house.

"Thank you. Head back to the office, Michael," I say to my driver.

"Yes sir."

"Okay, Mr. Machlin Saddler, in a few months you will officially be going undercover. Adam Klein the intern, welcome to the team," Elijah says with a laugh.

"Can't fucking wait."

Chapter 1
Genevieve

Six months later...

"Falon, where are the numbers for the Hawthorne Properties?" I ask, through the intercom on my desk.

"Working on them, Ms. Langston."

I log onto my computer and there's a soft knock on my door. My boss, Dillon Crenshaw comes in with a big smile on his wrinkled face. He reminds me of Santa Claus with his white beard, glasses, big belly and just as jolly.

"Busy?" he asks, taking a seat in the chair in front of my desk.

"Not too busy for you, what's up?" I lace my fingers together on top of my desk.

"We have an intern coming to work with us for the next month. He'll be working closely with you. Teach him the ins and outs of Saddler Enterprises, answer all his questions and make him feel at home. Sound good?"

"I..." I close my mouth before I say something stupid and then open it again when my brain restarts. "Of course," I say, with a tight smile.

"I know this is below your pay grade, but Machlin Saddler requested that you be the one to train him."

"He...he did?" I ask confused.

Why would Machlin Saddler request me to handle this? That asshole. What game is he playing?

"I speak very highly of you. There is no one else I would rather see molding the new employees, Genn. You know Rochelle and Elijah are behind you too." Dillon smiles and gets to his feet.

"Okay, well thank you, Dillon. I appreciate you singing my praises."

"Of course. He'll be here tomorrow. I'll send Falon in with his folder for you to review before he gets here."

"Great."

"Also...just giving you the heads up, Jeremy is going to be starting his training to takeover my position within the next few months."

I sigh and shake my head.

"Retirement is overrated, Dillon. Do you have to?" I ask with a puppy face.

He laughs as he walks to my door.

"Don't let him ruffle your feathers. We all know *you're* the one meant to be at the top, Genn. Keep that head up and ignore that little shit."

I laugh as Dillon leaves and Rochelle Saddler comes in a few minutes later with a folder, dropping it on my desk.

Rochelle is one of Machlin and Elijah's younger sisters, the CEO's of Saddler Enterprises. Rochelle runs Saddler's Startups which is a fixer upper branch of Saddler Enterprises. They mainly flip houses and she has become a great friend since I've started working here.

"This intern is hot!" Rochelle says, fanning herself.

I laugh and shake my head.

"Go for it, girl, he's all yours. You know I'm trying to--"

"Just focus on Kenzie. Got it, got it," Rochelle says, tossing the folder on my desk.

I open the folder and furrow my brows, studying his picture.

"This is hot to you? He looks like he belongs in an 80's porno. Who has a mustache like that anymore?"

"Have you ever had a man with a mustache go down on you, Genn? My Lord, it doesn't matter what it looks like, it *feels* amazing!"

"Oh Jesus. Well I'll give you his eyes. They're gorgeous. That shade of green is insane, it doesn't even look real. I am a sucker for a man in glasses though."

"This man is going to be on his knees in my office before the day is done tomorrow. Mark my words," Rochelle says winking.

"You're the worst," I laugh, looking through the rest of the folder.

"Okay Ms. Stick Up Her Ass. When's the last time you had a man on his knees? Your rule is for Kenzie to not get involved, but what about you?" she asks, crossing her arms over her chest.

"I...not that long ago maybe...a few months or something," I say, quickly averting my gaze.

"Genevieve Langston! Tell me my brother was not the only action you have gotten? That was months ago!"

"Just shush! Stop talking so loudly, dammit! I don't want to talk about this with you!"

"Oh, dear God. Okay, I will totally take one for the team and back away so you can experience a ride on Mr. Mustache. You need to. It should be on your bucket list, honestly--ride a mustache."

I laugh and throw my pen at her.

"Get out of here! I am not riding anyone's mustache!"

"Well, you can if you want! I'll go back to my fuckadex and leave the fresh meat for you."

"Fuckadex?" I ask, with confusion.

"Like a rolodex but with my men. It's organized into different sections and everything. If I'm in the mood for love making, I call Thomas. If I'm in the mood to get fucked six ways till Sunday, I call Axel. If I'm in the mood to suck dick, I call Kris. He has such a beautiful dick. If I'm in the mood to get my pus--"

"Okay, okay. I get it. You're insane, you know that?"

"Hey, I have a very healthy sex drive. Sue me."

"For fucks sake. Don't say sex, Rochelle. You're like what, sixteen?" Elijah interjects, from my doorway.

"Fuck off, Eli. I'm twenty-six."

I laugh when Rochelle sticks her tongue out at him, and he rolls his eyes.

"Do you two ever get along?"

"He's just mad because Mac is my favorite brother. He comes back tonight, wanna finish what you started?" She winks at me.

"Not funny," I snap, waving my finger at her.

"I meant a slap. That man deserves it. Maybe we can get all the Saddler's rounded up for dinner this weekend," Rochelle says smiling.

"Almost all them. I don't think we'll see Val until my wedding, to be honest," Elijah grumbles.

"Don't get me started on *that* nonsense," Rochelle says, rolling her eyes.

"Oh, shut it, Elle. Gretchen and I are getting married and we don't need anyone's approval," Elijah demands.

"See, that's her talking, right there. Already trying to weed out our family," Rochelle says, pointing at Elijah.

"Okay, I have an intern to prepare for. Can we pause the family drama and pick it back up at a later time? Preferably not in my office," I say with a smile.

"Sorry, Genn," Elijah says, shrugging his shoulders.

He waves and walks out and Rochelle follows before turning back to me.

"Drinks tonight at your place?"

"I'm gonna visit with my mom first, so probably not until 6. Good?"

"Oh Jesus, I'll bring the hard stuff."

I nod, letting out a sigh and she waves, walking out of my office closing the door silently behind her.

I look around my office and lace my fingers over my stomach as I lean back in my chair. It's still so surreal that I work for Saddler Enterprises. When MJ gave me his business card on that plane six months ago and I called to schedule a meeting, my mouth dropped to the sidewalk when I realized where I was.

Saddler Enterprises *is* Arizona. The biggest real estate company in the entire state. They branch out from commercial to residential properties, the section Rochelle runs, and they even have overseas accounts. That's where the infamous Machlin Saddler has been for the past few months, securing certain accounts in Spain.

Hearing the stories about his ruthlessness in business is one of the reasons I was dying to meet him. I wanted to pick his brain, learn everything I could from the genius that took a small startup company to the powerhouse it is today. How wrong I was to idolize such an asshole.

Genevieve

Five months ago....

I pace around the front of Elijah Saddler's house with Kenzie until I hear Rochelle's voice. It's been a month since my move and meeting Rochelle at work has been my saving grace. The Saddlers have been so kind and welcomed me into this company and their family with open arms.

"Hey, girl! Come on in!"

I smile, giving her a hug as I hand her the bottle of wine and brownies Kenzie and I baked for tonight.

"Full house, minus Val. She's in Europe somewhere, who knows where. You'll meet her when she resurfaces again."

"That's fine, I can't wait to meet, Machlin. I promise I won't fangirl," I laugh, nervously.

"Oh, he'll eat it up if you do, he's an asshole," she laughs.

We walk through the kitchen and I see Gretchen, Elijah's fiance cozied up to him and Dakota, the youngest of the Saddler's who I've met a few times. There at the end, sipping a tumbler of a dark liquid is pure perfection and dominance.

With styled, dark brown hair, a curl hanging lose on a tanned forehead, a hint of a five o'clock shadow coating his hollowed cheeks, and his eyes a beautiful shade of blue as they connect with mine is Machlin Saddler.

He is angelic perfection, wrapped with a devilish bow. The face of a man that could build you up, just so he can watch you fall to your knees.

An air of familiarity washes over me but it's gone quickly when I see his smile. What a dimple, my God.

"This must be our employee of the month. Genevieve, it's lovely to meet you. I've heard nothing but great things," he says, getting to his feet.

He walks over to me, kissing me on my cheek and I swear I momentarily forget to breathe.

"It's...so nice to meet you, too. I'm such a big fan. Your company has been a dream to work for and I love the infrastructure. The way you started is so inspiring and I...am rambling, sorry. I promised I wouldn't fangirl," I laugh, embarrassed.

"Come then, pick my brain," he says, eyeing me.

"Let's...eat first," Elijah says, stopping Machlin's descent on me.

"Of course," Machlin answers, with a smile.

I glance over at the rest of the crew and Dakota rolls her eyes as Rochelle tries to hide a smirk.

"Genevieve, why don't you come and help me grab a bottle of wine out of the cellar," Gretchen says.

I eye Rochelle and she points at me, laughing. I give her the discreet side eye as I follow Gretchen down the hallway to the stairs of the cellar.

"A little advice from someone who's been on the radar of a Saddler: stand your ground. These Saddler men have a persuasion like I've never seen but hold strong. They may be powerful, but they need someone to guide them," she says, smiling.

"I...I'm not on anyone's radar, Gretchen," I laugh.

"Machlin Saddler's jaw dropped when you walked in that room, Darling. He was trying to whisk you away before Elijah stopped him. Remember what I said," she says, grabbing a bottle as we make our way back upstairs.

Gretchen moves towards Elijah as the rest of the group heads towards the dining room and Rochelle stops me.

"What did that bitch say to you?" she whispers.

"I don't know, something about Machlin wanting me and Saddler men needing guidance. She's nuts, right? Machlin doesn't even know me," I whisper back.

"He probably does. You're gorgeous, he'd be blind not to think so, but like I said, he's kind of a dick. Love him, but he has to be that way, running a company and all."

"I...am not looking to date your brother," I laugh, nervously.

"Sure," Rochelle laughs back, walking towards the dining room.

We all sit, Machlin taking the chair next to me as he fills up my wine glass.

"You look beautiful tonight. If I knew my newest employee was as gorgeous as you, I might have cut my business overseas short," he smirks, clinking my glass with his.

There is that familiar pull again and I can't place it.

"This may sound crazy, but we've never met, have we? You just seem really familiar," I ask, studying him.

He turns away with a smile and shakes his head.

"I try to keep myself out of the limelight but maybe a picture has surfaced or something. Cheers. This is the best wine in our cellar, let me know what you think," he continues smiling, taking a long sip.

I follow his lead, shaking off the feeling and cut up Kenzie's food. I finally dig into my own and let out a soft moan when the flavors hit my tongue.

"This is phenomenal, Rochelle."

"Thanks girl. I'll give you the recipe."

"Please," I sigh, shoveling another bite in my mouth.

I take a long sip of my wine, feeling my nerves start to disappear at meeting Machlin, sitting next to him.

"You cook?" he asks.

"I do. I learned when I moved to NY. Tonya worked nights, so it was up to me to make dinner for us. I...don't know how much you know about me but Kenzie's mom was my best friend. She passed away and left me in charge and...I'm sorry I'm rambling again," I laugh tightly, taking another sip from my wine, trying to control the tears.

"I'm so sorry for your loss, but please, keep talking. I like hearing you talk," he says softly.

I search his eyes and my stomach drops. He's so handsome. I clear my throat and go back to eating, ignoring my body's insane reaction to him.

Once everyone is finished eating, Machlin stands, extending his hand out to me.

"Come outside with me for a little bit."

I look back at Rochelle and she nods, coming to lift Kenzie and bring her in the kitchen.

I nod to Machlin as he leads me away from the group, grabbing the bottle of whiskey off the bar and two clear tumblers.

"So...how's the company been treating you?" Machlin asks, pouring me a shot as we make our way to the patio.

He takes a seat next to me on the same lounge chair as me and I try to keep my excitement at bay.

"I...it's amazing. I love Saddler Startups, too. I'm so happy to be included in the showings and staging and everything

from start to finish. I've never been able to do everything before."

I drink down the shot, easing my nerves as I talk to the Machlin Saddler, alone.

"I'm happy you're enjoying it. You've had the biggest turnabout numbers I've ever seen in such a short time. How did they not include you on their team in NY? They must be nuts!"

He fills my drink again and I giggle, drinking it down. Slow down, Genn. Don't make a fool of yourself.

"Well, your employee I met on that plane, MJ, was my guardian angel. It's a shame he was transferred to the international offices. He...really helped me out that day," I say, remembering that kiss, the way he held Kenzie and gave me hope that I was doing the right thing and I would be okay. I still can't believe he was even real.

"He's a great guy. Has a knack for eyeing potential rockstars. I couldn't have picked a better employee out myself," he says smirking.

I laugh again and have to keep myself under control. God, I'm acting like I'm meeting Brad Pitt, although he kind of is. I've followed his company from the very beginning. The numbers, the growth, wanting that to be me one day.

"You're very flattering. I'm not gonna lie, I've heard some terrible things about you but you're nothing like what I've heard."

"Oh yeah? Do tell," he smiles, pouring me another shot.

"I really shouldn't have anymore. I drove and I have Kenzie..."

"I'll have a car take you home. So, what have you heard? Any of those things from that dickhead, Jeremy? Can't stand that guy," he states, shaking his head.

I finish my drink and point at him.

"Me either! God, he's a creep. Yeah, some things from him, kind of. He says you stay out of the spotlight because you're too busy fu--sleeping with um...a lot of women. You kidnap some, keep them in your big mansion basement...that kind of thing," I giggle.

His expression is serious and my smile fades.

"Oh God, I'm sorry. I don't know why I said that," I say, shaking my head.

He looks at me and his face breaks into a smile as he laughs. I let out a breath and giggle too.

"Is he kidding? I haven't even been on a date in God knows how long."

I look up at him and his smile falters as he looks down at my lips.

"I um...haven't either. All work and no play. I have Kenzie and I really don't want to introduce her to someone unless it's..." His face is getting closer. The alcohol invading my brain and Machlin invading my personal space is overwhelming.

Red flag, red flag. This is such a red flag. This is the CEO of the company you work for, Genevieve! Stop this! Stop this right now!

He puts his finger under my chin, and I tilt my head up.

"You intrigue me, Genevieve Langston. I want to kiss you right now."

33

"I...think I...wouldn't stop you," I whisper.

What the fuck am I saying? Word vomit. Stop!

His lips brush against mine, soft at first before they finally crash. He grips my head from behind, pulling me closer, our whiskey-soaked tongues tangling in a drunken, lust filled kiss. I lean into his touch with an intensity that should embarrass me, but it doesn't. I'm making out with Machlin Saddler!

His hands roam up my ribs and cup my breast and then my body goes cold.

"Is this okay?" he rasps. "Tell me not to stop."

"I...no this isn't okay, I'm sorry," I say pushing him off me. "I shouldn't have...let that happen. I got caught up and--"

"I was told you fuck as well as you sell houses, Genevieve. Do I have to earn that privilege to be the judge myself?" he asks, with a smug sneer.

My mouth drops open and I get to my feet.

"Excuse me?" I snap.

"Oh, come on. I'm better looking than that old hag you got fired in New York, aren't I?"

A bucket of ice-cold water has been thrown on me and I shake my head, closing my eyes to get my composure before I say something I'll regret.

"I never touched, Mr. Brighton. He sexually harassed three other women in that office, including me, and I won't be talked to like that by the CEO of the company I work for!"

"My apologies, then. I thought we were on the same page. I guess I have to judge you just for your sales then, not how long you can stay on your knees."

I scoff and toss my glass down on the side table with a crash.

"I think I should be going."

"Don't feel bad, Genevieve. Women find it very hard to resist me. You won't be the first and you won't be the last," *he smirks, putting his arm out for me to take.*

I blink a few times, my head reared back in shock. All this time I idolized a womanizing dick. What a disappointment.

"Right. Well have a good night and it was great to meet you," I say, with my fakest smile.

I turn away from him and walk back through the house towards the kitchen.

Rochelle eyes me as I motion towards Kenzie and she nods as I walk out the front door. I run a hand down my face, calming myself down and feeling like an absolute idiot.

What the hell was I doing? I'm a woman, I have needs but that does not include Machlin Saddler, especially after that encounter. God, what a fucking asshole.

"Ughhhh," I groan. "Idiot, Genevieve, all your hard work. Get it together!"

"What happened?" Rochelle asks, coming outside holding Kenzie.

"Can you drive us home? I can't drive."

"I'll drive your car home and stay over. Let me just pack up some stuff at my place, okay?"

"Yes, thank you."

We walk down the steps to my car as I buckle Kenzie in her seat and Rochelle starts it.

"What happened?"

"Your brother...he really is an asshole. He brought up Mr. Brighton from New York and basically propositioned me!"

"Fucking hell, I'm sorry Genn. I'll talk to him."

"No, don't, it's fine. Truthfully though, I might look for a new job. I'm so embarrassed and he's a nightmare."

"Please don't!" she pleads, putting her hand on my knee. "He's overseas a lot now anyway and I'll make sure he apologizes."

"Whatever. I'm an idiot. So much for picking his brain, I really wanted to have a serious conversation with him. All this time I thought he was a genius. I mean he very well could be but...I don't even care. It's like finding out Santa is really your dad's purvy friend."

"Oh God, that bad? I promise I'll talk to him."

I nod and lean my head back, letting out a breath.

"What a night."

Chapter 2
Genevieve

I step into the elevator downstairs to pick Kenzie up from childcare, trying not to think of the shitstorm I will be walking us into very soon.

"How'd she do today?" I ask Peggy, the head teacher.

"Excellent! Not one accident!"

Kenzie runs up to me and I kneel, wrapping her in a hug.

"My big girl! No accidents today?" I say excitedly.

"Me potty!"

"I think someone gets ice cream tonight!"

Kenzie claps and kisses my cheek before turning and hugging Peggy goodbye. I take her backpack from the floor and we hold hands on the way out of the office.

Tonya was having a hard time potty training her, as she just turned three right before Tonya was killed. She has to be fully trained before pre-school and missing Tonya has put her back a few steps. The women in the childcare center here are so understanding though, and slowly Kenzie's getting the hang of it again.

"We're gonna go see LeeLee okay?" I tell her as we walk towards the car.

I strap Kenzie in the backseat, taking a deep breath before starting the car, knowing full well that my mother is going to put a nail in the coffin of this day.

I drive the twenty minutes out of the city to her house and see her rocking on the front porch, a beer in her hand.

At least it's after five o'clock this time.

"Okay, big girl, we'll see LeeLee for a little and then Auntie Elle is gonna come over, sound good?"

Kenzie claps her hands and we walk up the drive to the porch, my mother not even turning to greet us.

"Hey Mama, it's Kenzie and me. How's your day been?" I ask, kneeling in front of her, putting my hand on her thigh.

She doesn't even flinch, continuing to rock and stare out in the distance.

"Mama?"

She shakes her head and looks down at me, but her expression doesn't change.

"Genevieve? Is that you?"

"Yeah Mama, it's me. I'm here with Kenzie. You remember Kenzie, right?"

"Where is your husband?"

"No Mama, Kenzie is Tonya's little girl. I'm not married."

She takes a long drink, sitting the beer back on her thigh and I exhale.

"Mama, how about I get you a glass of water instead, okay?"

She shakes her head and stands, wobbling a little on her feet.

"I just want to sleep. Put me to sleep."

I nod and motion for Kenzie to follow us into the house as I drape my mother's arm around my shoulder, walking her to her bedroom.

I lay her down, pulling the blanket over her body and kiss her forehead.

"I love you, Mama. Get some sleep."

I pull the shades closed and shut the door behind me as I make my way out to the kitchen with Kenzie. It's a disaster; bottles of beer and liquor strewn about on the counter and I have no idea how she's even getting it. I make a mental note to talk to the neighbors and hope they're not the ones bringing it to the house for her. Grabbing a trash bag from under the kitchen sink, I start cleaning, dumbfounded at the mess she can make in only two days, the amount of alcohol she drank during that time.

She's getting worse.

From the day I came back to now, she hasn't been herself. Hell, even the day I came back, I barely recognized the woman that raised me.

She's thin, frail and depressed. She won't see a doctor and the few times I've sent someone over, she's told them she'll shoot them if they step on the porch.

My heart hurts at the realization that I may not be able to help her. I wrack my brain for some idea of how to get her out of the house, even just on a walk, trying to regain some sort of normalcy without alcohol.

My father was her life. High school sweethearts that traveled the world together and then they had me. The house, white picket fence and the little girl; we had the perfect life. I remember it so clearly. We were always happy, smiles on both of their faces and then he was killed in the line of duty one night and everything changed.

"Me clean, too?" Kenzie asks, pulling on my leg.

I shake those thoughts out of my head, wiping a stray tear and bend down to Kenzie, giving her a smile.

"You're such a good girl. You wanna help?"

She nods with her cute little smile and I kiss her cheek, sitting her on the counter.

"I'll wash, you dry, okay?"

She nods enthusiastically as she grabs the dish towel and I get to washing the dishes.

An hour later, I check on my mom one more time, leaving a glass of water by her side and some Advil. I kiss her on her forehead and close the door behind me, locking the front door on my way out.

"Ready to see Auntie Elle?"

"Auntie Elle, Auntie Elle!" Kenzie chants.

I laugh as we drive back to my three-bedroom bungalow style house.

When I first moved back to Arizona, we stayed with my mother, but I quickly realized it was not the place to raise Kenzie. Rochelle brought me to one of their fixer upper homes that was close to being done and we bonded over our love of decorating. She helped Kenzie and I move into it and we've been inseparable ever since. She's so good with Kenzie and gave me a friendship I so desperately needed after losing Tonya.

I pull in the driveway and Rochelle is waiting on the porch, a pitcher in one hand and a brown bag in the other.

"You're a lifesaver, I owe you homemade ones next week," I groan, smelling the food from our favorite Mexican restaurant.

"I figured you didn't want to cook after seeing your mom. How's she doing?" Rochelle asks, as I open the front door.

"Not good. I'm at a loss of what to do."

Kenzie climbs on top of the kitchen chair and I lay out a taco on a plate for her. Rochelle pours us both a margarita and I take a long sip.

"I just can't even imagine loving someone so much that you just totally disintegrate when they're gone. Is that even a real thing?"

"I...I d-don't know, never felt something like that," Rochelle stutters, shrugging.

"That's a bunch of BS if I've ever heard it. You got all stuttery. What the hell are you hiding?" I smirk, crossing my arms over my chest.

"Some people experience loss differently, that's all. Some wallow, some...explore."

She takes another sip from her drink and I eye her.

"Explore, huh? Is that what you do with your endless fuckadex? Explore? Who's the guy? What happened to him?"

"Nothing happened. No guy, I just...realized men suck and they're only good for one thing. Story over."

"Better to have loved and lost than not loved at all, right?"

"Now, I call bullshit on that one, it's better to just fu-- sleep," Rochelle says, eyeing Kenzie.

"Fine, fine. I'm not getting anything out of you then, huh?"

"No ma'am. Let's eat and get drunk. I brought clothes to crash."

Machlin

"You're sure about this, right?" asks Elijah for the tenth time, as I sit on a chair in front of a mirror in my office.

No, I'm not fucking sure about this. It's a terrible fucking idea but I have no choice.

"Can you stop asking me that. I'm doing it, end of discussion," I snap, instead.

"Just...Genevieve is really going to be pissed at you for this, ya know? I don't understand why it has to be her?"

"Elijah, she works with Jeremy on every damn sale. If I can get close to her, I can get close to Jeremy. I'll get her to trust me and we can work through it together."

The woman behind me starts fussing with my hair and I flinch. This is going to be annoying as fuck.

"I don't get why we can't just bring him in the office and question him. Hire a private investigator?"

"Because I don't want to spend money on a private investigator. That asshole took enough!"

"I make enough money while I take a piss to pay a private investigator. Why are you being so cheap?" Elijah scoffs.

"Because I want to be the one to catch that lying fuck! Any more questions?" I yell.

"Ahh, it's a pride thing then, huh?" Elijah asks, sitting down in the chair next to me.

"I'm sorry I raised my voice, but yes, it's a pride thing. I put my blood, sweat and tears into this company with Dad and I won't stand for someone stealing from it, tarnishing his memory. I want to be the one to nab this piece of shit and then we can all move in the right direction."

The woman fusses with the wig on my head and I already feel it starting to itch.

"There isn't another wig? I'm going to go fucking nuts with this on my head for hours on end," I complain.

"N-No sir. The rest are even fuller than this one. Anything s-shorter and people might recognize you," the women stutters.

"Fine, what else do we need?" Grumbling, I lean back in my chair.

"Facial hair, green contacts and glasses. Luckily most people here have minimal contact with you, but like I said, Genevieve will be pissed. You guys made out, what makes you think she won't recognize you? What about your voice?" Elijah laughs. "Especially if you plan on getting close to her. What if she kisses you? She'll know it's you."

"No, she won't. I'll kiss different or some shit. Besides, the plane was almost seven months ago, and at your house, she was too busy hating me and a little buzzed to even register how I kissed. I'll make my voice a little higher, it'll be fine. She's exactly where she needs to be. Hating Machlin and ready for nice guy Adam to sweep her off her feet."

"And why exactly does she have to hate you?" Elijah asks with confusion.

"Because then she'll run from the worst man right into the arms of the best one."

"I still don't understand why you have to be such a dick to her. Are you sure it's for this whole undercover boss thing or is it because she makes Mr. Grinch realize he has a heart?"

I glare at him and grit my teeth, knowing full well that's exactly the reason. If I keep her at a distance, hating my guts then she's safer there. Despite her fire when I'm around, she's broken. I'll break her even harder. They'll be nothing left of her if I let her get close to me. I was put on this earth for one reason; to take care of my family, not to fall in love.

"Grinch is thinking about it?" Elijah laughs, snapping me out of my thoughts.

I flip him off and shake my head.

"She'll get close to Adam, we'll nab Jeremy, and all's right in the world again. It's not like she'll fall in love with the guy, it'll be a friendship...kind of."

"And Rochelle won't even know? Our own sister? Have I mentioned how fucked up this is?" Elijah says, shaking his head.

"You have and I've mentioned that I don't really give a shit. Now, let's finish this so I can start this whole charade. Four weeks is way too long."

Trying to pretend I haven't thought about Genevieve every damn day since that plane ride is going to be the hardest thing of all.

Chapter 3
Genevieve

A strong knock on my door breaks me out of my work fog. I look up and see our intern, Adam Klein. He's in a black suit with a green tie and he walks into my office with a bright white smile and a man-bag over his shoulder. Jesus, where did this guy come from? I walk towards him, my hand extended for our introduction.

"You must be Genevieve Langston. I'm Adam Klein, it's nice to meet you. I'm really excited to be working alongside you. This is a great opportunity for me."

"Hi, Adam, it's great to meet you, too."

Our hands touch in a handshake and I feel a jolt straight up my arm. I pull it back quickly and notice he does it too. *He felt it.* His crazy green eyes bore into mine behind his glasses and a knock at the door interrupts our stare down.

"Sorry to bother you, but, oh hi! Is this our new intern?" questions Rochelle from the doorway, a smug smile on her face.

"Adam, this is Rochelle. Rochelle, this is Adam. Rochelle runs Saddler's Startups. If at any point you want to learn a little bit about how that's running, let her know. I'm sure she'd be thrilled to show you the ropes, right Rochelle?"

"Ropes, chains, cuffs, I'm not picky," she says, winking.

Adam coughs and clears his throat and I give Rochelle the stink eye. She puts her hands up in defense and walks out, leaving Adam and I alone.

"Sorry about her, she's really flirty. There's not a no fraternization policy in place, so I mean...she's...friendly. I'm sure you'll get the gossip around the office because nothing is really a secret. She's an amazing girl and if you want to be the one to try and lock her down, be my guest," I laugh.

Adam is staring at me, mouth dropped open and I shake my head.

"I'm sorry, too much for a first day. How about we just focus on the job part and later you can work on the social part...by yourself."

"Right, yeah," Adam says, shaking his head.

He smiles and there's a familiar pull in my belly. He's actually...cute. Rochelle's voice about riding mustaches echoes in my head. I focus on his mustache, his tongue shooting out and licking his lips as he clears his throat.

I snap my gaze up and shake my head.

"Sorry, I...am being a little unprofessional. I've...had a long day," I laugh, nervously.

I walk around to the other side of my desk and motion for Adam to sit. My brain is so jumbled right now; worrying about all the craziness in my life and Rochelle's words are not helping matters.

"One second," I say, putting my finger up.

I take out my phone and send a quick text to Rochelle.

Genevieve: All I'm thinking about now is riding his mustache. I hate you.

Rochelle: Supply closet on the 2nd floor is open and has a lock. You walk in first, wait five minutes, then he joins. Works every time. If you don't bring him there, I will.

Genevieve: Stop it!

Rochelle: Use your power, tell him to get on his knees! Or get on yours, whatever tickles your taco.

Genevieve: That's sexual harassment, Rochelle! Tell me you don't do that.

Rochelle: Of course I don't...

I groan and throw my phone on my desk and look up, getting myself together.

"So, tell me about you, Adam. What made you want to work for Saddler Enterprises? The real estate world?"

He smiles, an adorable smile, and takes his bag off his shoulder, leaning forward on my desk.

"Well, I used to build things with my father. He was really handy and anything that needed to be fixed, my mother would make a list and he would fix it. Once I was old enough, about 3 or 4, he let me help. First thing I ever built was a doghouse for our new pup. I fell in love with being able to take nothing and make it something...a home."

"That's...that's how I feel about it too," I say, smiling.

"Yeah? It's amazing, isn't it?"

"It is, yeah."

We stare at each other and he clears his throat, looking away.

"Anyway, I graduated from Arizona State like it says and here I am, hoping to start my career here."

"So you're...twenty-two then?"

"Yes, ma'am."

"You...can just call me Genevieve. Ma'am makes me feel old, which I am. I mean I'm older than you. Four years older than you, too old for you," I blurt, quickly.

He laughs and shakes his head.

"I don't think that's too old for me, I mean not that there's a we but...yeah.... Well, how do you like working for this company?" he asks, leaning back in the chair.

"Thank you for that...change of subject," I laugh. "I swear I'm not this weird and awkward, I'm...just having a day."

"I don't think you're weird or awkward at all," he says smiling, our eyes locking again.

I swear this feeling of familiarity hits me, but then it's gone as Adam shakes his head and breaks the spell.

"So, this company is amazing. I love working here and they acknowledge hard work. I started six months ago, and I've moved up relatively fast. I did work in the real estate world in NYC, so my experience helped, but if you put in the work, you'll be rewarded."

"That's great to hear. If the employees are happy then the company thrives, in my opinion."

I nod. "Of course. I mean it's not without issues, don't get me wrong. Elijah is a big part of the company but there's also Machlin. He's not around a lot, I've actually only met him a handful of times. He's...an acquired taste, I guess. He runs a lot of the overseas accounts but it's nice to interact with who you work for on a daily basis."

"Sounds kind of like a stuck-up jerk," Adam grumbles.

"He can be ruthless, sure, but you kind of need that in a CEO, I guess. It would just be nice to put a face to the name more often. I mean you also get a little 'all work and no play' kind of thing. It's hard to take vacation. I've had a week saved up, but it would be more work for me to take the week and come back to my huge pile of accounts, than just stick it out and not take a vacation."

"That's gotta be frustrating. Why can't someone else take over your accounts while you're gone?" he asks, leaning forward.

"We cater to the client. If they have me on their account, they want me from beginning to end. That's what sets us apart from other companies. We don't pass around clients like a game of hot potato, we stick with them and gain their trust. Our main source of business comes from recommendations."

"Sounds like a great infrastructure for the clients, not so much for the employees," he says, furrowing his brows.

"I'm making it sound terrible to work here!" I laugh. "It's really not bad, I just...I have a little girl. My best friend passed away and left me as guardian of her daughter, so it would be nice to take her on a vacation. If you're single without responsibilities, it's really great."

"I see," he says, eyeing me. He smiles and nods. "I am single, was that you fishing for info?"

My mouth drops and I shake my head.

"That was not me fishing, but okay. I...I'm single, too."

I blush and shake my head with a smile as I look down at my desk.

"I...don't really date, though. I have Mackenzie to look after, and I don't want to bring just anyone into her life."

"Understandable," he says, lifting his hands in defense. "I think it's admirable of you, taking on a child that isn't yours. I'm sure your friend would have been very happy that you honored her wishes."

I bite my lip, willing the emotions to stay put and nod.

"She would have, yeah. Anyway, why don't we uh...figure out what's first. You can learn a lot in a month, I don't want to brag but I'm a great teacher."

"Well I can't wait to learn."

"You did great today. You picked up the system super-fast. What did you think?" I ask, as we walk out of my office and I turn to lock the door.

"Honestly? It wasn't as hard as I thought it would be."

Adam shrugs as we walk towards the elevator and I smack my hand to my forehead.

"Shit, I forgot my phone in my desk and the Graham property folder. I'll catch you tomorrow?"

He nods as the elevator opens and I wave, walking back towards my office. I unlock the door and head towards my desk. Reaching inside the top drawer for my phone, I check it, making sure there are no messages and slip it into my bag.

I ruffle through a few folders on my desk, trying to find the folder for the property we're working on tomorrow and sigh.

"Shit, where the hell is it?" I groan.

I search through my folder files and accidentally knock down one of the frames on my desk. I lift it up and come face to face with my dad and me out on the lake fishing when I was about ten. Our smiles are big...so happy and I remember my mother taking the picture and almost falling into the lake as she walked backwards to get a better angle.

I laugh, feeling the tears start to form and look up, blinking them away.

"Dont, Genn. Don't go there."

"Talking to yourself now?" asks a man from the doorway.

I turn towards the voice and gasp, my hand going to my chest.

"Jesus Christ, you scared the shit out of me," I complain.

"Machlin Saddler actually, sometimes people get confused though," he says with a smirk, putting his hand out for me to shake.

He's in black slacks, a white buttoned-down shirt with the top few buttons unbuttoned and no tie around his neck. His hair is a mess and it's so unlike him to look this disheveled and it's...hot. Dammit.

His hand is still extended for a handshake and I walk up to him, slapping it down and grit my teeth.

"I don't find you funny. Is there something you want?" I snap, my sadness gone, replaced with annoyance.

"Besides you bent over my desk? I could go for some dinner. You?"

"Ha! Like I'd go to dinner with you!" I scoff.

"I said I could *go* for some dinner, didn't say I wanted to have dinner with *you*," he says, shaking his head.

"Wow, and here I did my senior thesis on Saddler Enterprises. Little did I know their CEO was a pretentious prick. Have a good night, Machlin."

I brush past him and he grips my wrist, stopping me.

"How's the intern?" he asks softly.

"He's fine. Really good actually, but it's only day one. I...thank you for suggesting I be the one to train him. I hope you're not giving me this responsibility because you think you're going to cash in a weekend in my bed," I say, pulling my wrist from his grasp and crossing my arms over my chest.

"Nonsense. Why would we go to *your* bed when I have a California King Beautyrest?"

I roll my eyes and walk towards the hall, waiting for him to join me so I can get the hell out of here.

"How is HR not waiting to shave your eyebrows off with the amount of sexual harassment fires they probably have to put out because of you!" I say, slamming my door shut and locking it.

"Ms. Langston, I only sexually harass *you*," he smirks, walking closer to me.

"That's not funny, Machlin. I'm being serious. Stop this."

I put a hand up to stop him, pushing against his hard chest.

"I'm playing with you, Genevieve, it's what we do. You pretend you hate me. I remind you how much I want to fuck you and you pretend you don't want that too: Lather, rinse, repeat. Actually, that doesn't sound half bad. Care to join me?" he asks, putting his hand out.

I smack it away, groaning as I stomp towards the elevators.

"You're impossible. Don't take the elevator with me, wait for the next one," I say, pushing him back as he tries to step inside.

"Scared you'll end up half naked on the security cameras?" he whispers.

"No, petrified of wearing orange. It's not my color," I say with a wink as Machlin laughs, as the elevator doors close in front of him.

I let out an exasperated breath and shake my head. That bastard. He's the only person on this damn planet that can get under my skin.

"You really don't have to stay. You've been killing it the past few days. You were made for this," I say, smiling at Adam.

"No worries. If you're staying, I'm staying."

He smiles as I hear buzzing and he reaches inside his pants to fish out his phone.

"Sorry about this. Mind if I step out?"

"Not at all."

He nods and walks towards the door and I admire his butt in his dress pants.

God, I really need to go on a date.

I focus back on my work and Adam comes back with his face twisted in an annoyed expression that's pretty adorable.

"Everything okay?"

"Just family stuff. I...I have a few younger sisters and...it's just tough. When they hurt and I can't do anything about it, I just feel...useless," he says, exhaling.

I study him and my heart starts to constrict, the strings getting pulled by Adam's caring side and I need them to stop. Instead of ignoring it, I push, because I'm a masochist, apparently.

"I am a woman, anything I can do to help?"

"She's just...had a rough first love. She likes to keep moving instead of dealing with the fallout. I hate that she won't come home but...too many memories, I guess. I mean I get it," he says, dropping down to the chair opposite my desk.

"That's got to be hard. First loves are tough to get past. You wonder if you can ever trust someone again," I say, playing with a pen on my desk.

"You sound like you're talking from experience," he replies, causing me to snap my gaze back up to him.

I give him a small smile and nod.

"My high school boyfriend. We split before college, figured we couldn't do the whole long-distance thing. At least that's what he said when he left. I mean, he didn't cheat on me, hurt me, and wasn't nasty to me. He was really a great boyfriend, I just thought he would have asked me to follow him. I didn't have my mind made up about where I was going to college yet and was open but...he didn't."

Adam nods, reaching over the desk to cup my hands.

"His loss. You're a great woman, Genevieve."

"Thanks," I smile. "It's fine, really. I decided on NYU, met Tonya and had a lot of time to focus on school. I had my job lined up before I even graduated, so it worked out."

"That's really impressive. Graduated..."

"Summa cum laude," I state proudly.

"Wow. Here you are, constantly impressing me."

Our eyes lock and I glance away, trying to rid the feelings he keeps stirring up in me. He's so tempting; his personality, his kindness. He would make a great partner and I mentally smack myself for thinking it. *Too soon...way too soon.*

"What about you?" I ask, changing the subject instead.

"Graduated magna cum laude," he smirks, rubbing the back of his neck.

"That's still impressive. What about the girlfriend?"

He scoffs and shakes his head.

"She uh...got caught up in wanting to be a trophy wife, I guess."

I narrow my eyes at him, and he clears his throat.

"Obviously, that's not me so...ya know. We parted ways."

He speaks too quickly, and I wonder briefly if he's lying. He doesn't look at me, but it could be out of embarrassment. I'm sure it's not easy having a woman leave you because you're not as successful as she hoped.

"Well, that's really shitty. Ya know what? This conversation needs a pick me up. We can work on this stuff tomorrow. They have a great little cafe downstairs with the best ice cream sundaes. You want to try it?"

He smiles. It's a big, breathtaking smile and then nods, getting to his feet.

"I think that's exactly what we need."

Chapter 4
Machlin

I walk through the hall of Saddler Enterprises bright and early with two iced coffees and a chocolate cake donut.

Genevieve's door is open, so I turn the corner and head towards it, but stop when I hear voices.

"Ya know, I'll need you available to me 24/7, Genn. I'll be the new Dillon soon," says a male voice.

"Jeremy, I know what my responsibilities were to Dillon and being your personal assistant was never part of my job description. I have my own clients and my own things going on, you just oversee it," Genevieve responds, in a hard voice.

Good girl, stick up for yourself.

"Okay then, how are things going with the intern?"

"They're going great. His name is Adam, by the way."

"Adam, huh? He's young, no? Fresh out of college?" Jeremy asks, in that smug fucking tone.

I know exactly where he's turning this conversation and he better fucking not.

"Yes, he is. He knows what he's doing though," Genevieve says, oblivious to his motives.

"He's a little young for *you*, no?"

Okay, enough is enough. I walk into Genevieve's office as her mouth is on the floor, staring at Jeremy.

"Morning team. How are we doing?" I ask, with a smile. "Iced caramel coffee and chocolate donut, right, Genny?"

I see Jeremy's head snap to Genevieve, and he gives her a hard look but then turns to me.

"Morning, Adam. How are you today buddy?" he asks with a fake smile, patting my back.

"Great *buddy!*" I say back, with just as much fake enthusiasm as I can muster up, patting his back with double the force he used on me.

He coughs, his eyebrows raising at the contact and I smile, sitting down in the chair opposite Genevieve's desk.

"Well, I'll leave you two to it. We'll catch up on those closings a little later, Genn."

She nods at Jeremy as he leaves the office and I see the stress on her face.

"Why are men such...jerks?"

"Hey!" I laugh, motioning to the coffee and donuts.

"Sorry, not you. You don't count. Thank you for this, I needed it."

"Can't have my boss in a bad mood. Forget about him. Jealousy is an incurable disease. He knows you're pulling in double his numbers and will probably run this floor soon."

She furrows her brows at me, and I curse myself for spilling all that info. Fuck. I can't think around her, dammit.

"I...ran into Machlin on the way up. Those Saddlers really have your back," I say, with a laugh.

"Ha! Machlin?" she laughs sarcastically. "Not a chance. He doesn't think about anyone except himself."

"You don't like the guy, huh?" I ask, sipping my coffee and going in on my donut, trying to keep my mouth busy before I spill something else.

Let's hear what you really think of me, Ms. Langston.

"Truthfully, he's a genius. I mean, I followed his company from start to finish. He gave me hope that it could be done. It's my dream to one day run my own real estate company. Crazy, I know," she says, shaking her head.

"Not at all. What's life without a few dreams?"

She looks up at me and smiles. I see so much of myself in her; optimistic, eager for more. She's fucking intoxicating.

"Exactly. I mean I talked to him, hoping to pick his brain, but I was too excited and nervous. We ended up kissing, it was a disaster. He...just made me feel like an idiot. Don't tell anyone this, okay? It's so embarrassing," she grumbles.

Fuck, my chest. What is happening to my chest right now? I feel like I want to throw up and my body aches. I...*feel bad*. Shit, I feel so bad. She slung hate right back at me, I didn't know I actually hurt her, embarrassed her. I let out a sigh and shake my head.

"Well, he's an idiot for treating you like every other girl. You're nothing like anyone I've met before," I say, softly, word vomit now that I can't turn off.

She looks at me, our eyes lock and she smiles.

"Thanks Adam, that's...incredibly sweet."

I can see her cheeks pinken just the slightest and it's the cutest fucking thing I've ever seen. This was a mistake, this was such a fucking mistake. The more time I spend with her, the more I realize this plan sucks. Yes, I'm getting more access to the closing documents that she sits in with Jeremy on, but I'm also getting to know Genevieve, and this can't happen because I'm starting to really, really...*like* her. God, I need to stop, but I can't. I can't stop myself and I keep pushing.

"So...Machlin's still top grade asshole to you?"

"I don't see him much, actually. He is usually away on business. We have big accounts in Spain and when he's here, he just sticks to the top floor, thank God."

"He never comes down here? Strange, no?"

"Rarely. I think it's only to bug me, to be honest."

I try to hold in my smirk as she continues. I do like bugging her. That little scowl on her forehead has become something I look forward to seeing.

"Elijah and Rochelle do more here. He should check in more often, though. Sometimes people run a little rampant," she says, taking a bite of her donut.

"What do you mean?"

I perk up at that little bit of info, sitting up straighter.

"Well...not to be a gossip or anything, but Jeremy takes ridiculous lunch breaks. He always checks in with me before he goes, trying to convince me to eat with him and most of the time he's gone 2, sometimes 3, hours. He pretends he's on a work meeting, but I check the schedule and there's nothing on there."

"He sounds like a snake," I say, my anger rising.

"He is. I have my eye on him. I don't trust him, but don't worry, I'm not some brown-nosing kiss ass. I just have a bad feeling about him. I keep to myself, do my work and leave everyone else alone, but him...there's just something about him."

"Did you tell anyone? Elijah, Rochelle, even Machlin?"

"Not yet. I don't want to come off weird, especially to Machlin. He'll probably brush it off like I'm obsessing over him or something. I am going to tell Elijah though, when I figure out what's going on."

"You don't think he's...stealing from the company, do you?" I ask.

Her head snaps to me and her eyebrows pull together.

"I...shit do you think he is? I'm always on closings with him. I've never noticed anything weird on the documents though, I always double check."

"Well, has he gotten a new car lately, worn better quality suits? New watch? I don't know, what are warning signs?" I ask, trying to play it cool.

"I'm not sure, I'll have to dig a little. I mean he showed me the new watch he bought the other day but...damm. I hope he's not, but I wouldn't put it past him," she says, shaking her head.

"Well, I'll help you keep an eye on him," I state, getting to my feet.

"Sounds good. Anyway, you ready to stage your first home today?"

"Already? It's only been a few days," I laugh.

"Sink or swim, Klein. Up and at em!" she says, getting to her feet. "I don't like to stage in my nice clothes, mind if I change quick?" she asks, walking towards the bathroom in her office.

"Of course. Take your time."

She closes the door behind her, and I walk around her office, glancing at the pictures on her desk.

There's a picture of her with Kenzie and another woman who I assume is Tonya. Kenzie is sandwiched between the two women's cheeks, a cute little smile on her face and my heart pulls. How hard it must be to raise a little girl that reminds you so much of your best friend. They looked so happy.

"That was a few days before her accident," Genevieve says from behind me.

I jump and turn around quickly.

"I didn't mean to snoop."

"It's okay, it's on my desk so it's not snooping," she assures me, smiling.

"You must miss her a lot," I say softly.

"I do. I really do. We um...were roommates in college. After we graduated, it was only fitting that we stayed together. She was a nurse, working the night shifts in labor and delivery. There was more money there and she wanted to switch, but then she got pregnant. The guy was a dick-- didn't want anything to do with her or Kenzie--so we worked out a system. She stayed on nights so I could work during the day and then be home with Kenzie at night. She didn't want to put her in daycare, and I didn't mind. She was a great baby and I was there when she was born. It was crazy! Kind of made me never want to have a baby, to be honest," she laughs, looking down at the picture.

"I truthfully don't know how Tonya did it, though. Working all night then watching Kenzie all day. She barely slept. The company I worked for didn't have the childcare they do here, so we really didn't have a choice."

She takes a big breath and lets it out.

"They said it was a wrong way driver, there was probably nothing that could have stopped it but...I don't know. Maybe if she was more alert, she would have swerved a different way or seen it earlier or..."

She wipes at her eyes and I walk closer to her, pulling her in for a hug.

"You can't dwell on that, Genny. I believe that things happen for a reason and although it's such a tragedy, it could have been worse. Kenzie could have been in the car, too. I'm sure Tonya is looking down on you both and she's happy and proud at how well you're taking care of her little girl."

She nods, hugging me back and then breaks it, wiping her eyes with a sad smile.

"Thank you, Adam. Sorry for breaking down like this. I'm usually okay but it'll hit me at random moments."

"I understand, believe me."

Thinking about my parents now, I have to collect myself. I can't confide in Genevieve about them, it'll be too obvious. I swallow the knot in my throat, not allowing myself to go there. I haven't gone there since the day I got the phone call five years ago. Take a breath, let it out and move on.

She walks around the other side of her desk to grab her purse and her outfit is the distraction I need. Suddenly, my head is clear, and my burden is lifted.

"Should I change? You look like a teenager going to a ball game and I'm your sugar daddy," I laugh, motioning between us.

I'm in my black suit and tie and Genevieve has changed into cut off denim shorts with a black tank top, a flannel tied around her waist and her brown hair in a high ponytail.

She laughs and rolls her eyes.

"You heard Jeremy's comment I'm guessing? The age thing doesn't bother me, you don't have to say that."

"I'm serious, Genny."

"And so am I, Adam," she laughs. "But no, you don't have to change, unless you want. We're not moving big things today, I just feel more comfortable when I'm just Gen the stager, rather than Genevieve the associate broker."

"Fair enough, I can't wait to watch you work," I wink.

Her cheeks redden again as she shyly looks away, walking towards the door and I follow.

"So, my mantra is always light and bright. Buyers want to make sure that their home will get plenty of natural light. Make sure curtains are pulled to the sides, shades open, all that good stuff," Genevieve says, as she walks around the living room opening blinds.

It's hard to focus on light and bright when all I feel is horny and hard. Every time she bends forward, I swear her ass is going to pop out of those shorts, or if she bends towards me, her tits will. I can't focus on anything else and I keep walking away to adjust myself.

Damn dress pants, they hide nothing. This woman has been my undoing in more ways than one. Elijah's words keep circling in my head. This is just attraction, nothing more. It's been awhile since I've had a woman and I'm a warm-blooded man.

"You okay?" she asks, as she looks up from rearranging magazines on the coffee table.

It takes all of me not to glance down her tank top and I give her a tight smile, shaking myself out of my own thoughts.

"Yep, just...learning."

She eyes me with a suspicious gleam in her eye then looks back down to work. I'm a weak man and I look too, and I swear I see a nipple. She unties the flannel from her hips and wipes her forehead with it, tossing it to the couch.

"You're not dying in that suit?" she asks as she turns around, giving me her back.

She bends down, reaching for something inside the box and I get a quick glimpse of a tattoo on her lower back. A *tramp stamp. She has a fucking tramp stamp.*

"Jesus Christ," I groan.

She stands and turns around, putting her hands on her hips to study me.

"What is the matter, Adam? Is this too much? I'm trying to go slow I just--"

"Truthfully? Your clothes are distracting me. I...can't concentrate on anything else except you," I grunt, watching her gaze slowly drift down my body to my unhidden erection.

Fuck, Adam wouldn't have been so crass like that. This is shit Machlin would say. *You run a multimillion-dollar company, asshole, get your shit together.* I open my eyes again, ready to apologize and see her eyes widen slightly.

"I'm sorry, I shouldn't have said that, I--"

"No! No..it's my fault, I normally don't have anyone with me when I stage. I didn't think about my attire."

She smirks a little and I groan.

Liar. God, she is such a tease. I can see the mischief in her eyes. She wants to break her no dating rule and she wants to break it with me. A stronger man would be able to resist, but if she coaxes Adam, turning her down would push her away from him, right? I need her close to me--to Adam. I'm a selfish shit, who am I kidding? I've wanted her for months.

"Is that so?" I ask, walking closer to her. "Or were you trying to get a rise out of your intern? See if you could get me to force your hand? Break your rule?"

She walks backwards until her back is pressed against the fridge and the coolness of it makes her buck forward, right into my chest.

"No I...that's not what I was doing," she whispers, her eyes dropping to my lips.

I shouldn't be doing this, I *really* shouldn't be doing this, but I need to. For me and for the company, I need her close. My dick needs her close, dammit.

"Well, I want you to, Genny. I want you to break your rule...for me."

I move my face closer to her and our lips are a whisper away.

"I...can't," she says, lightly pushing on my chest.

I back up as she closes her eyes and groans, throwing her head back.

"God, I want to. I really, really want to, Adam, but I...have Kenzie to worry about. It's a lot but, if things were different..." she says, shaking her head. "I'm sorry if I gave you the wrong impression. I like you. I do and I really, really want to kiss you but...I'm sorry, I'm not making sense, I'm all over the place, I..."

I laugh and walk over to her, wrapping her in a hug.

"I get it, I do. I'm sorry if I made you uncomfortable."

"Not at all, really. Let's just forget it," she says, waving her hand away.

"Forget what?" I laugh.

She smiles, takes a deep breath and we walk further into the kitchen as she tells me how important flowers are when staging a home, and how clutter is the devil.

Shit. Way to go bud, way to go.

Chapter 5
Genevieve

"I almost kissed Adam!" I groan, as Rochelle walks into my apartment.

"You didn't! Wait, you said almost? Why the fuck didn't you!" she yells, putting the wine and takeout on my counter.

I texted her as soon as we got back to the office for emergency takeout night and haven't stopped thinking about that "almost kiss" since.

"We were staging a house and I was in my staging clothes and he was so...hot! He kept checking me out and the look in his eyes...uhhhh like he wanted to just eat me whole. He was hard and had me against the fridge and I stopped him!" I groan, throwing my hands in the air.

"Oh my God, Gen! What the hell is wrong with you? I'm leaving, tell that man to get his ass over here and fuck you senseless," she says, getting to her feet.

"No! Don't! Rochelle, I can't! I can't do this with him! The company means a lot to me."

"Oh, stop! What the hell does the company have to do with anything? You're pulling at straws! You date...maybe break up and he works at the same place. Why is that so terrible?"

"I don't know, what if he broke my heart and then has a new girl at the office. I have to watch them be all coupled up and stuff. What if I broke up with him and he's a clinger and I can't ever move on? Workplace romances never work, I can't do it."

"I think you can, you're just scared. Stop being a little bitch and go for it," she says, taking out our food.

I watch as she unpacks everything, and I think about her words. Am I scared? What the hell do I have to be scared of? Kenzie comes barreling through the kitchen and jumps into Rochelle's arms.

"Hello, my little princess, you ready to eat?" Rochelle asks.

There's my answer. *Kenzie.* It always comes back to her. She's never had a man in her life, how would she react if I started bringing one around? How do I even start that? Do I wait until I'm super serious with someone and engaged? Do I bring him around quick to weed out if he likes kids? She seems to like Adam, whenever they see each other. Does he want kids?

"Your head is going to explode, stop thinking so hard," Rochelle says, handing me a glass of wine.

"I'm so confused," I grumble.

"Well, I'm not. He's hot. If you're throwing him back into the wild, I'm snatching him up."

"Have you even had a conversation with him?"

"I don't need words, I need action."

"You're the worst, I like him Rochelle and you're my friend!"

"But you're not doing anything about it."

"Jesus, you have enough men!"

"There's never too many. Eat and shush."

I roll my eyes and dig into my food, thinking about Adam and Rochelle. I can't not want him but then stop someone else from wanting him, it's not fair. But I do want him, dammit. I think...maybe? Dammit, dammit, dammit.

"Unless...does my brother have anything to do with this?" she asks, wiggling her eyebrows.

I choke on my food and grab my wine, taking a big sip before speaking.

"What the hell does that mean?"

"Oh, please! The heat level on your sexual chemistry puts this damn desert we live in to shame," she laughs.

"I...that's not...I hate him, Rochelle. *Hate*."

"Do you know what kind of sex people who *'hate'* each other have? Mind blowing sex. Get it over with and then decide on Adam. If you can't kiss Adam without picturing Machlin, there's your answer."

"I don't picture...I..."

Shit, did I? No! Adam is sweet and caring and kind. Machlin is a complete dickwad. A hot dickwad though. A really hot dickwad. Thinking about all the steam he stirs up in me, unleashing all that against a wall in the office or--

"Yep. You need an anger bang. Only solution."

I go from a dry spell to a tsunami, how the hell did this happen?

I carry a sleeping Kenzie to her bed and stub my toe on a Lego on the floor. I grit my teeth, holding in my reaction and mentally drop every curse known to mankind.

I gently put her into bed, pulling her mermaid comforter over her small body and move her hair out of her face, smiling.

"You look so much like your mama," I whisper, holding back my tears.

I kiss her forehead and walk out of the room, wiping at my eyes. I walk down the hall to my room, shedding my clothes as I climb into bed.

I fiddle with my phone, hovering over Machlin's number and then Adam's. I know eventually a male presence in Kenzie's life would be good for her, but which one? I briefly think of MJ from the plane. He was so good with her. There are good men out there, I just don't know who to trust.

"Give me a sign, Tonya. Tell me I'm doing this right. I'm trying so hard to give her everything you would have."

I fold my hands over my belly and exhale as I shut my eyes and try to get some sleep.

"Hi slugger," says a familiar voice as I stand on the front lawn of my childhood home.

"Daddy?" I turn and see my father with his big, broad smile with his arms open and I run to him, jumping into his arms.

"I've missed you, my girl," he whispers.

I feel my eyes start to water as I grip him with everything I have, not wanting to let him go because then I'll lose him again.

"Daddy, I miss you so much. I miss you so, so much," I sob.

"Shh, it's okay my girl, it's okay. Everything is going to be okay. You're strong, remember?"

"I don't feel strong, Daddy. Tonya is gone and Mama is slipping away from me. I have Kenzie and I...it's a lot. It's all a lot," I sob harder, burying my face into his chest. "I need you. I need you so bad right now."

"Oh, my girl. You carry around all this weight. Let it go. Tonya is grateful to you. Kenzie loves you and your mama will be okay. You're doing a great job, Genevieve, but be happy. Don't lose your happiness trying to give it to everyone else. They'll create their own from the love you give."

I nod and wrap my arms tighter around him as I feel him slipping away.

"Don't, Daddy. Please don't go yet. Not yet, please," I beg.

I'm soaking his shirt with my tears, my knuckles white with my grip.

"Sleep my girl, get some rest. I love you with all my heart, Genevieve Anne. All my damn heart, slugger."

He vanishes and I'm startled awake as I put my hand over my chest and still my rapid heart. I move it up to my mouth and catch my sob as it shakes my body with loud, hurt cries as I remember the feeling of my father's hugs. I'm slowly forgetting how it felt and I lay down, hugging my pillow as my cries slowly subside. Too much...this is all too much.

I try to go back to sleep but I can't, torn between wanting to see my father again but knowing it'll break my heart again if I do. Eventually, exhaustion wins but I don't see him in my dreams again. I see...Machlin.

Chapter 6
Machlin

I watch Genevieve work as I lean back and pretend I'm doing the same. Organizing accounts that I can easily do in my sleep. She intrigues me, which I knew she would as soon as I laid eyes on her holding Kenzie on that plane. I can't stop thinking about her and I need to. Too many people rely on me, I don't need to add two more to the list.

"So, when do you break for lunch?" I ask.

"In about an hour. I was actually going to have lunch with Kenzie today."

"She stays at the childcare here every day, right?"

She looks up and I see her studying me, trying to figure me out and I give her a disarming smile.

"Yep. It's on the first floor."

"That's a great perk to have for working parents."

"It is."

She looks down again, going back to work and I stand. Clearly, the "almost kiss" has got her bothered, but I need to continue on and make her comfortable with me again, plus she looks...sad today and I don't like it.

"Anything bothering you?" I ask.

"I...no, I'm fine. Just a lot on my mind, that's all," she says with a tight smile.

"I can finish up if you want to go down and eat with Kenzie, take an early break. I don't mind eating by myself," I say, shrugging.

"That's really not necessary. You can...come and eat with us, if you want? It probably won't be a quiet lunch though, if that's what you're looking for," she laughs.

"I'm actually one of f--four, I don't mind the crazy," I say laughing, kicking myself for almost giving her a big clue.

There's a knock on the door and Rochelle comes in while sporting her wide, flirty smile. I cringe in my seat and look away. I'm going to have a nice talk with Elijah about our baby sister.

"Came to break the new guy in. Want to go get lunch, hot stuff?"

I try to hold the bile down and look at Genevieve as her jaw flexes. Hmm, interesting.

"He's actually going to have lunch with Kenzie and me," she says with a strained smile.

"Is he now? Kid guy?" Rochelle asks, as I turn and look at her.

Her arms are crossed as she leans against the door frame.

"He's one of four, loves them, right Adam?" Genevieve asks, looking at me.

I nod and watch a smile creep up on Rochelle's face.

"Claws away, Genny. He's all yours. Just testing a theory," she says winking.

"That's...no, I...you're more than welcome to join, it's not like that," she stutters.

I see Rochelle study me and then the moment of recognition hitting on her face as her mouth drops open.

"Actually," I say, getting to my feet. "Maybe lunch with Rochelle is a better plan. I'll be back in an hour," I say quickly.

I guide a shocked Rochelle out of Genevieve's office, not looking back until we hit the elevator. We stay silent as other employees' pile in and her brows are furrowed, shaking her head at me as I press the button for the top floor.

We wait a few seconds as the elevator ascends and walk out on the executive floor, towards the back offices.

She pulls me into her office and shuts the door behind her, slapping my chest.

"What the fuck is this? God, you have no idea! I wanna vomit right now! I said you were hot! I told Genn to ride your mustache! I said *I* wanted to! I...oh God, I'm gonna throw up!" she groans, walking to her bathroom and splashing water on her face.

"She doesn't know, no one here knows except Elijah, Rochelle. There's been money missing. I needed to figure things out and this was really the only way without alerting everyone," I say, walking towards her bathroom.

"Undercover boss type shit? Mac, she's gonna be hella mad at you! She already hates you!"

"I know, I just...she has to understand it's for the company. I suspect Jeremy and she's the only one that closes with him. I think I can find out more info, I just need another two weeks, finish out the month. Don't say anything to her, please," I beg.

"Mac, you're asking for a lot. She's become one of my best friends and I think she's crushing on you! The Adam intern you and the *you*, you!" she says, slapping my chest.

"Elle, you have no fucking clue. Ever since that plane ride, I...just, I don't know, I can't describe it. Not saying anything at that dinner and pretending I hadn't met her before. Working with her every day, almost kissing her, I'm going fucking nuts ov--"

"Wait!" Rochelle says loudly, putting her hand up to stop me. "Plane guy! You're plane guy, too? Fucking shit, Mac! How did you get away with me not finding that out? Does Elijah know?"

"Yeah, he knows, I told him to keep an eye on her. I figured you guys would get along, I didn't want to put you in a weird position if you knew."

"And what the hell do you think is happening now? This is worse! God, I hate you sometimes, Mac! Why did you have to do this undercover shit with *her*?"

"Elijah suspected Jeremy and they work closely together. If something is going on, I'll be able to get it through her."

"Genevieve is the best employee we have and a rule follower. Why the hell would he confide in stealing money from the company with her?"

"Not a straight-out confession, but she has access to all their closings together."

"Don't you have that? You're the fucking CEO!"

"Yes, but I don't look at closing documents. If I fish around for something like that, it'll send up a red flag to the board. I want to do this as quietly as possible."

She lets out an exasperated sigh and shakes her head.

"I hate this, just so you know. Two more weeks and that's it, then I tell her! I'm not kidding around, Mac. She's going to feel so betrayed."

"I'll find a way to smooth it over, don't worry about that, okay?"

She rolls her eyes and I smile, shaking my head.

"You dig mustache guys, huh? Kind of weird little sister."

"Shut the fuck up, Machlin Saddler. Don't you dare tell anyone about any of this or I'll kill you in your sleep!"

I laugh again and walk out of her office back towards the elevators and to Genevieve.

Rochelle is right, Genn's going to hate me. Not only is she going to feel betrayed, but she is going to think the only reason she moved up so fast in the company is because of the plane ride. She can't know about that part yet, maybe not ever. She'll hate me even more than she already does. It won't matter though. If she hates me, she's better off. I'm not capable of softening my exterior for anyone; kindness is weakness in this business and in life.

I think back briefly to my parents, how loving and caring the both of them were. Life never handed them any breaks. We lost our house when I was ten, renting out two bedrooms in a run down shack on the outskirts of town. All four of us slept in one room, while my parents had the other. I remember sharing a kitchen and bathroom with my parents, all my siblings and the four other people living in the house.

At first it seemed fun, like a hotel, until I could see the look on my parents' faces, the stress that covered their happy smiles. Finally, my father was able to secure a trucking job and my mother started to clean houses. We were able to move to our own two-bedroom house and I was to take care of Elijah, Valentina and Rochelle.

School was not an easy feat either. The "sorry" Saddler siblings that wore raggedy clothes and never invited anyone over their tiny house. Sports were too expensive, so we had to wait until school started to join a team. Realizing the school didn't provide equipment, we had to quit and find a different way to take up our time after school.

That's when Val, Elijah and I came across a thrift store on our way home one day. There were so many hidden gems and I came back the next week with my lawn cutting money to buy a few. I worked on each piece in my room, using stuff around the house to make them brand new again. Once I thought they were perfect, I brought them back to the thrift store and sold them for twice what I paid.

I brought the idea to my father one night. Seeing as he always built things, fixed stuff around the house anyway, I asked him to allow me to not only fix things but change them around a little bit. My mother found out she was pregnant with Dakota and our two bedrooms would not be big enough for the seven of us now, so he agreed.

I spent every waking moment on that house; sprucing up old fixtures, sanding furniture and painting every inch until it was sparkling, almost brand new. My father got in touch with a real estate agent and we sold that house for three times what we paid. There was a local college that was being built so the area was booming, the market extremely hot.

My parents bought us a gorgeous five bedroom house and from there, my father invested in a "fixer upper" business. I worked with him after school, on nights and weekends and soon, Elijah and Rochelle started to show interest as well. Rochelle was always interested in our projects when she was younger--swinging a hammer before she could even walk--so it was only fitting she helped, too. Within months, Valentina took pictures of our first "fixer upper" and we sold it, turning a profit.

My father took Saddler Startups to the next level, then I built Saddler Enterprises from the ground up. It took years of my life, working 90+ hours a week until we were *it*. When my father passed away, he left all of Saddler Startups to Rochelle, since she was the sole Saddler working with him. Everything I have ever known is hard-work and family. There is no room for anything else in my life when I have four younger siblings to take care of in my parents' absence.

My father's letter to me in his will was my driving force these past years, and it doesn't leave room for a distraction. Genevieve Langston is just that--a distraction. She shuts off my worries, the burden I have on my shoulders and I can't have that. That can never be shut off. I need that reminder every damn day.

Chapter 7
Genevieve

Holding Kenzie's hand in the elevator we make our way to my office, still mulling over the whole exchange with Rochelle and Adam.

Since he's started here, he's seemed annoyed every time she's come to chat but I'm not the type of woman to fight over a man, especially with my best friend. I brush it off as Kenzie pulls on my hand.

"Whats up, baby?"

"Go up?"

I glance over at the elevator buttons and notice that we are going up and sigh. I'm so distracted that I didn't even press the button for our floor.

"Yeah, sorry, baby. We'll be back down in a little. Need to pick up the big guys," I say smiling, pressing the button for our floor.

We stop at the executive floor and the doors open as my jaw drops.

Adam. Rochelle brought him up to her office. His eyes widen too and he gets inside, giving me a small wave.

"Hey, just...had to discuss something with Rochelle."

I give him a tight smile and nod as we take the elevator down in silence...awkward silence.

"Hi, Man," Kenzie says, breaking the awkwardness.

"Hey, Kenzie! How are you today?"

"Good, Man," she says smiling.

"I decided to actually order in, if that's what you guys are doing?" Adam asks, from next to me.

"Sure, sounds great," I say, pushing down the jealousy.

Rochelle is my friend, I told her I wasn't ready to date, and we discussed this last night. I really didn't think she'd go right for him, though, I should have no reason to be jealous. God, my brain is going to explode. Too much is going on right now, I don't need these stupid feelings on top of it.

We get to our floor and Adam lets Kenzie and I walk first as we head down the hall to my office. I turn the knob and catch Adam's gaze go from my ass to my face and I roll my eyes. This isn't the first time I've caught him ogling me, even staging the house wasn't the first time, but it doesn't flatter me today, it annoys me.

He probably just hooked up with Rochelle after trying to kiss me the other night and now he's checking me out again? What an asshole, just like Machlin. So much for my kindness theory. Men are all the same. I'm on edge today from my dream about my father, my feelings towards Adam, my super inappropriate dream about Machlin...everything piling up and I feel it all about to break. I need to take a breath, but my annoyance wins.

He catches my expression and shakes his head, walking into my office behind Kenzie.

I shut the door and set Kenzie up in the corner with her coloring books and crayons before walking to my desk and dialing for takeout.

"Deli?" I ask, looking to Adam.

His eyes are on my tits now and I slam the phone down.

"Okay, I tried to be cool, but this is ridiculous. If you want Rochelle, that's fine. I told you I wasn't ready to date so I get it, I do. Even though I like you, a lot, and probably would take a chance and do dinner with you if you asked because that almost kiss was...forget it, that's not the point," I say, shaking my head. "If you're going to be with Rochelle, then know that we're really good friends--best friends--and I won't allow you to shamelessly check me out after you've just been with her. She deserves better than that and so do I. I'd appreciate it if you stopped."

A small smile forms on his lips and I cross my arms over my chest.

"What the f--" I eye Kenzie in the corner and take a deep breath. "What is so funny, Adam?"

"I'm not with Rochelle, I'll never be with Rochelle, but that dinner invitation intrigues me," he says, getting to his feet.

"I...what dinner invitation?" I stutter, as he walks closer.

"The one that I'm going to ask you to and you're going to say yes."

He's close now, our chests almost touching, and his hand goes to the back of my head, pulling me closer.

I eye Kenzie but she's coloring, oblivious to what's about to happen.

"Wh-what if I say no?" I whisper.

He runs a thumb down my cheek and smiles.

"I won't stop asking until you say yes."

"You're...not with Rochelle?"

"I'm not with Rochelle. The only woman I want in this building is *you*, Genevieve."

The way he says my name as he looks into my eyes, like I've heard it before, maybe in my dreams...maybe...no. He has blue eyes, not green. God, my head is messing with me. Rochelle's damn voice creeping into my head again. Adam, not Machlin, dammit. Stop thinking about him!

"Okay," I whisper.

"Okay?"

I nod and he pulls my face closer, our lips about to touch before there's a knock on my door and it opens.

"Oh God, sorry," Rochelle says, clutching her chest.

I jump back like I've been burned and my cheeks heat with embarrassment.

"I...had something in my eye, Adam was..."

She puts her hand up to stop me and her hard gaze lands on Adam.

"Remember that *thing* we discussed, *Adam*," she says, through clenched teeth.

"Very well, actually and I think I can handle it on my own, although your input was appreciated."

I see him stiffen and I close my eyes, shaking my head.

"Rochelle, he said you guys weren't a thing, I'm not trying to get in the middle of--"

"We're not," Rochelle says, cutting me off again. "Believe me, we're not, nor will we ever be. Ever, ever, ever. Never ever." She lifts her finger to point at Adam and furrows her brows. "Think before you act! Come find me later, Gen. I have to ask you something."

She turns and shuts the door behind her, and I turn towards Adam.

"What...I'm super confused. Did you do something to her?"

"No! We just...didn't see eye to eye on something, that's all. I promise, nothing is going on with Rochelle, okay?"

I nod and sit down at my desk as Adam takes his seat across from me.

"Come to dinner with me tonight?"

"I...don't have a sitter for Kenzie, it's super last minute," I say, lifting my phone to dial for takeout.

Adam nods a sad nod and I order, watching his expression as he turns and walks towards Kenzie with a smile. He sits next to her, taking out some crayons as they color and when I hang up the phone, I hear her contagious giggle.

"That's not the color of the grass, silly girl,"

"Me like!" Kenzie says, pointing to her picture.

"I like that, too. Okay, we'll leave it."

Adam turns and we smile at each other.

"How about you come over for a late dinner tonight? I can make something or order takeout? Is that...too forward?" I ask with a laugh.

"Just dinner sounds good," he says smiling. "I can pick something up on the way."

"Okay, thank you."

His cellphone rings from his pocket and he stands, glancing at it.

"I need to take this. Sorry."

He walks out of the office and I go back to my desk, finishing up some paperwork as Kenzie colors.

A few minutes later, Adam comes back with a regretful look on his face.

"I have to go, family emergency. But I'll still be able to do dinner tonight, if you want?"

"Sure, of course. Everything okay?"

"It will be."

He takes his bag off the chair and walks over to Kenzie, saying goodbye as he gives me a wave and leaves, our almost kiss quickly forgotten.

After Kenzie and I eat lunch, I bring her back down to the childcare room and head back up to my office, ready to plow through some work without having to stop and explain everything I'm doing. Adam has been a great help, but it's kind of easier when he's not around.

I think about our dinner tonight and smile. How quickly everything can go from stress and sadness to...excitement.

Before the elevator doors can close, a hand stops them and they open. I grit my teeth and will my body to stop the stupid reaction it always has towards this infuriating man.

Machlin Saddler...again.

His cocky smile knocks me on my ass and his smell takes over the entire elevator. He walks inside, the two of us alone as we take the ride up.

"How are you today, Genevieve?" his smooth voice coos.

I swear his voice is so sexy he could probably make me come just from saying my name. It's deep and raspy, like silk against my skin. My brain doesn't exist when he's around and I have to remind myself I have Adam coming to my apartment tonight. Nice, safe, charming Adam. Fuck Machlin Saddler. No! I meant don't fuck him.

"Great," my tone clipped.

"You still don't like me very much, do you?" he says laughing.

I choke on my words, coughing a few times and then finally collect myself to answer.

"What in the world gave you that impression?" I laugh, sarcastically.

"I can just tell. Every time I see you with that 'I hate you, but I want to angry fuck you' look on your face. It's so sexy and I might stop this damn elevator and make it come true. Lick that sexy little tattoo you have and make my way lower."

My jaw drops at his words and I cross my arms over my chest. You would think I'd be used to his crass comments.

"This is exactly why I said not to get in the elevator with me last time. I cannot believe you just said that to me!" I gasp.

"It's true, is it not? Right now, you want to hate me but I'm sure your body is telling your brain to shut up so it can take over. Right. Damn. Now. No?"

He turns towards me and I stumble back.

"Again, that's probably something an *employee* shouldn't say to another *employee*, especially a CEO! God, you are an asshole."

"I'm honest. I want to fuck you too, don't worry. It's not one sided. I don't just go around kissing and propositioning any woman I meet."

He turns back to the elevator door and I shake my head.

"Listen, the first time I was really drunk when that--"

"No need to explain, Genevieve. You're spoken for now, I get it."

"Spoken for? No, I'm not spoken for. God, what century are you from?"

"I'm trying to abide by your rules. No dating, right?"

"I...well yes, but I actually have a date tonight with Adam. I guess the right man can make me reconsider my position."

He turns and gives me a shocked expression and I smile, loving that I'm able to throw him off guard.

"Adam, huh? Guy looks like a serial killer. You should be careful."

"Your company hired him. Shouldn't you know that?" I question, crossing my arms over my chest.

He turns and looks at me, giving me a smile.

"Of course he's not. He's just the perfect man, isn't he?"

He stalks towards me, caging me against the wall, our chests bumping together. My breathing picks up and I try so hard not to focus on his lips.

"How did you know about my tattoo?" I whisper.

"I have my ways. Try not to think about *me* when you're kissing *him* tonight," he whispers in my ear.

Shit, Rochelle, you jerk! I close my eyes and grit my teeth but before I can lash out, the elevator stops and Machlin is gone.

I step out of the elevator and it's like everything comes crashing back at me. For the briefest moment, I forgot about the weight...the responsibilities, the sadness. Why does Machlin Saddler have to be the one to do that to me?

Chapter 8
Genevieve

I pace around my kitchen wondering what the hell I am doing. Why did I invite him over here? It's been forever since I've been on a date, I wouldn't even know what the hell to do.

"Shit," I whisper.

The last guy I kissed was Machlin and that was a freakin' disaster. The doorbell rings, breaking me out of my thoughts and I shake them away, pulling out all the confidence I possibly have in my 5'3 frame.

"You got this. It's Adam. He's the nicest guy on the planet and he likes you, so just cool it," I whisper to myself, as I walk to the front door.

I open it and smile as Adam stands before me in jeans, a t-shirt, a bottle of wine in one hand and a pizza box in the other.

"Wasn't sure what toppings you liked on your pizza, so I just kept it plain cheese. I should have asked, I'm sorry."

He walks forward, giving me a kiss on my cheek and his mustache tickles me. I laugh and shake my head.

"It's okay, I'm not one for toppings. Plain is fine, come on in."

He walks through, straight to the kitchen and sets the bottle and box on the counter.

"I hope you like red, too. I didn't do a very good job on my first impression date," he grumbles.

"I-I'm nervous too," I whisper, taking the bottle from his hands. "It's been a super long time since I've done this."

I reach up to the top cabinet for glasses and struggle until I feel a hard body against my back and ass.

"Let me," he whispers.

That raspy, hoarse voice pulls at something inside me and I turn, studying him while our faces are inches apart. Before I can really put my finger on it, his lips crash into mine and I flinch, leaning my back over the counter. His hand comes behind my head, steadying me and his other rests on the counter next to my hip.

I gasp when I feel his tongue slip into my mouth but then my hand is running through his thick hair, keeping him in place, allowing him to tangle with my tongue.

He takes my hand off his hair, bringing it down to his neck and I run my thumb along his jaw as his body adjusts to mine, pushing me harder into the counter.

"I didn't come here with the intention of this," he pants, breaking our kiss.

"I know you didn't, but keep going," I pant back, grabbing his face to lock our lips again.

I haven't been with a man in almost a year and I know I should stop this. I know it's going too fast and I will. In a few more seconds, I will definitely stop this.

He lifts me in his arms, sitting me on the counter as he moves his body flush against mine, his bulge against my inner thigh. He's an amazing kisser, and again I have that familiar feeling tingling up my spine when he breaks it, pressing soft kisses up my neck instead.

"I hope my honesty won't scare you off but you are the most gorgeous woman I've ever kissed, Genevieve."

His hand finds my hips as he pulls me forward more, pressing my center directly into his and his lips are back on mine again. Stop this, I was going to stop this, wasn't I?

His hand moves down to the top of my ass, lifting my body so he can squeeze it. Shit, what is one night? Kenzie already knows him from work and now she's sleeping. I can indulge for a night, can't I?

No, you can't, Genn! You are technically his boss. You're older than him and totally robbing the cradle right now. If this was high school, you'd be the cougar senior, making out with the little scared freshman.

Adam pushes his body into mine harder and I feel his length push against my clit. But this isn't high school, and he is so not a scared little freshman.

"Mustache," I pant, as he takes a long lick up the side of my neck.

"What?" he asks, pulling his face back to look at me.

"I...I meant..."

"Let's eat," he says with a smirk.

"I...I thought we...were...going to eat," I say, with a smirk of my own.

"I want to take things slow with you, Genevieve. There is no denying I would take you right against this counter and...let you ride my mustache," he says with a smile, eyeing his erection that is clearly evident. "But you deserve more than that, plus Kenzie is here. We don't want her to get a show."

I nod, hopping off the counter and smack myself for fooling around with Adam out here in the open. As if on cue, Kenzie stumbles into the kitchen holding her blanket and teddy.

"Oh, baby girl, what's the matter?" I ask, lifting her in my arms.

"Hi, Man," Kenzie says, taking her thumb out of her mouth to wave.

"Hi cutie. Would you like some pizza?" Adam asks, taking a small slice out of the box.

Kenzie nods and I watch as he cuts it up into pieces then hands it over.

"Here ya go, cutie. One pizza, hot and fresh."

He gives her a smile and I see her return a shy one of her own. I feel myself blush at how charming Adam is and can't help but touch my lips, missing the feeling of his on them.

We eat in silence, Adam and I both stealing glances at each other as Kenzie eats on my lap. She finishes her pizza and lets out a loud yawn.

"Tired little lady?" I ask, kissing her cheek.

She nods and buries her head into my neck.

"Say goodnight to Adam."

Kenzie leans towards Adam and opens her arms, wrapping him in a little hug. She leans into him, out of my embrace and Adam laughs, catching her.

"Okay, cutie. Let's go to bed."

He gets up from his chair and nods towards the doorway as I walk towards Kenzie's room.

Adam carries her so naturally and my ovaries are currently combusting in fifteen different directions.

"You have such a beautiful room. Fit for a princess," he whispers, laying her down in bed and poking her nose.

She lets out a giggle as Adam pulls the covers over her small body and she cuddles her teddy bear.

"Night baby girl," I say, leaning down and giving her a kiss.

Adam and I walk back towards the kitchen and Adam pours me a glass of wine, clinking our glasses together.

"Want to...sit in the living room?"

He nods and I turn, walking to the loveseat. I sit and Adam follows, taking the seat right next to me, our thighs touching.

Adam smiles, patting his thigh and I raise my eyebrow.

"Foot rubs make up for not knowing what color wine you drink and what toppings you like on your pizza," he says smiling, reaching for my foot.

I laugh, throwing my head back as he digs his thumb into my bare foot.

"I'm super ticklish, I don't know how this is going to work!"

Adam laughs, a rough, throaty laugh as he slides his hand higher up my calf, massaging my leg and I moan, my laugh dying in my chest.

"God, that feels amazing."

"Better first impression?" he asks softly.

"Yessss."

"So, you have any other tattoos besides the one on your lower back?"

I open my eyes and look at him with a smirk.

"Did that turn you on?"

"It might have. I normally don't act on my desires like that. I seem to not be able to control it around you. I apologize if that was too much."

I laugh and shake my head as he continues to massage my legs.

"That's the only one and I got it when I was sixteen. My mother caught me fooling around with a boy and didn't allow me to go to his prom. Just to be the brat I was, I let him tattoo me in spite of her. He was older and worked at a tattoo shop."

"Oh, I bet she loved that," he laughs, pinching my toe.

I laugh and slap his hand.

"She hated it! I pranced around the house with a crop top making sure she saw it! Told my father she was taking me to get it removed the next day," I say smiling, playing with the string on the throw pillow, remembering that not long after that, he was taken from us. The memory of him from my dream the other night, still so fresh in my mind.

"How'd you get out of it?"

"My dad said if I could beat him at 'horse' I could keep it. We used to play all the time; it was kind of our thing."

"Basketball, huh? I would have never guessed."

"He wanted a son and got me. Took me fishing, taught me how to build things, sling an axe. He's uh...kind of the reason for my love of the real estate world. My mother wasn't one for decorating, so I'd get an idea in my head and he'd build it. We built my whole bed frame from scratch. I still sleep on it."

"No way! I need to see this," Adam says with a smile.

"Trying to get me to invite you into my bedroom, huh?" I smirk.

"You're right, you're right. Next time," he responds with a wink.

"Anyway, I always like staging the best out of everything. Finding things that people see as trash, bring it back to life and add it into each house. I always gift it to the person that buys the property. Anytime I make something, I always think of him."

Adam stares at me, his mouth hanging open and my smile fades. I clear my throat and let out a nervous laugh.

"Anyway...what about you?"

"I...yeah, I mean, I..." he trails off.

"I'm sorry, I didn't mean to make the conversation sad."

He puts his hand on my knee and I look up, seeing his expression change.

"You never have to apologize for talking about your father, Genevieve. Believe me, I can relate to your pain."

I cover his hand with my own and squeeze it.

"I'm so sorry, Adam. Loss is never easy."

"No. No, it's not. I've had siblings to help me get through mine though, having no one must be difficult."

"Well, I had Tonya since my freshman year in college and my mother for a while before she...well before she became what she is."

"What happened to her?"

"She uh...drinks...a lot. Stopped taking care of herself, the house...everything. I didn't realize how bad it was until I moved back here. I...don't know how to help her and it kills me," I say, sighing.

"There's only so much you can do, Genevieve. People deal with loss differently. Just being there for her is all she needs."

I nod, wiping away a tear.

"Kenzie keeps me going, truthfully and Rochelle has been a great friend, Elijah too. The Saddlers really are great people."

"Aside from the asshat, Machlin, right?" he smirks.

"I'm sure he is in his own way, I just...don't see it," I say shrugging.

"Well you can add me to your list. I'm here anytime you need me."

"And that goes both ways," I say with a smile.

Adam nods and stands, putting his hand out for me to take.

"I should get going, my boss is kind of a hardass and she requires coffee bright and early or she becomes bosszilla."

I scoff and slap his chest, rolling my eyes.

"I think she'll let you off the hook tomorrow if you give her a proper goodbye kiss."

I stand on my tippy toes as Adam moves his face down, pressing his lips softly against mine, cupping my cheek. He pulls back, locking his gaze with mine and smiles as his thumb rubs my cheek.

"Goodnight, Genny."

"Night, Adam."

Chapter 9
Machlin

"I ran through all the numbers again and nothing makes sense. He had to be working with someone else because the sales line up and so do the commissions," I grumble, as I sit across from my brother in his office.

"You think the tip we got was falsified?"

"No, it was a real close. I fact checked it. What the hell are we missing?" I groan.

My brain is all fucked up today, working all night on the info I grabbed from Genevieve's computer while she was at lunch with Rochelle.

"Did you look into who the bank sends for closings? Is it a woman?" Elijah asks.

"I think ..I'll check that. I wouldn't put it past fucking scumbag Jeremy to seduce the poor girl. Why didn't I think about that?"

"Because your head is so far up Genevieve's ass," he smirks. "Or maybe you wish it was."

"Shut the hell up, it is not. It's my job, Elijah. I'm doing my job," I say, rolling my eyes.

"Of course you are."

I don't believe that lie how the hell am I supposed to make anyone else believe it? I'm in such shit. There's a soft knock on the door and Elijah tells the person to enter and there's the reaction my body has...Every. Damn. Time: lust, need, desire, want, hunger. God, I want her so bad.

"Genevieve! What brings you up here?" Elijah asks, getting to his feet and walking over to her, kissing her on her cheek.

"I just wanted to ask you about the Buckley account. It was supposed to be just mine but then I saw it got switched over to Jeremy. Is there a reason? I've worked with them on their last two purchases, I hope they didn't ask for a transfer?"

She's worrying her lip and her vulnerability is rare, especially around me. She doesn't show weakness around me...ever. Something weird happens in my chest and I want to make her feel better. Her insecurity is *hurting* me.

"Not at all. We uh...have something we need Jeremy to do for us and the Buckley account will satisfy it if that makes sense, which it probably doesn't, but you did nothing wrong so don't worry," Elijah says with a smile.

"Okay good," Genevieve says, letting out a breath. "Scared me for a second!"

She finally looks over at me and her expression changes from playful to fire. It seriously turns me on like nothing in my entire life when she slings that hate my way.

"Hello Machlin," she seethes, saying my name as if it's a disease.

I give her my charming smile and stand, walking closer to her to kiss her cheek like my brother did. She gasps, stepping back and shoots daggers at me.

"It's nice of you to finally acknowledge me."

"It's not all about you, Machlin," she says, crossing her arms over her chest.

"No, no it's not. I promise I give as well as I receive," I say with a wink.

"You're a pig," she seethes, rolling her eyes and turning to leave.

"Have lunch with me," I say quickly, running up behind her.

"I have a lunch date with Adam," she answers with a smug smile.

Is it crazy for me to be jealous of myself? I thought I would be able to get her to break the date, but I guess not. Damn.

"Do you now? Does that poor guy know that when you're with him all you think of is me?" I ask, moving a strand of hair off her face.

She smacks my hand down and grits her teeth, *growling* at me. She fucking *growled* at me.

"Fuck you, Machlin," she whispers.

"Believe me, baby, I'm trying to get you to, but it's really, really *hard*."

I give her a sly smile and she moves closer, our noses touching.

"And I plan on making it even *harder*."

With that she whips around, turning towards the door and walks out, slamming it behind her. I exhale, my body tensing at her exit.

"Oh brother, you are in a big pile of shit with her," Elijah says shaking his head.

"You have no idea."

Genevieve

God, that asshole! I hate that in just a few minutes in the same room, he can rile me up this much!

I was *not* thinking about Machlin last night! At all!

I stomp downstairs towards my office and fling open the door, headed to my desk to get some work done before Adam gets here.

I'm curious and nervous how work will be today after our date last night. I know we need to try and keep things professional at work, but do we kiss hello? Do we joke and show affection?

Stop overthinking this, Genevieve.

I'm an hour deep into my work when Adam strolls into my office, coffee and breakfast in hand and a big smile on his face.

"Good morning, beautiful. How did you sleep?" he asks, leaning over my desk to plant a kiss on my lips.

It's quick and easy as he sits across from me, unloading the food.

"Good. I slept good," I say with a smile.

"Me too. Good dreams," he says with a wink.

I laugh and roll my eyes, digging into my breakfast sandwich.

"So, what's on the agenda today? Besides of course me continuously admiring your beauty."

I laugh and shake my head, taking a sip of my coffee.

"You're too much. We have a closing soon, unfortunately with--"

"Knock, knock," says Jeremy from my doorway, walking right inside my office.

"Perfect timing," I grumble. "What can I do for you, Jeremy?"

"Came to pick you up for the closing. Want to grab something to eat on the way?"

He sits in the chair next to Adam, completely ignoring him and it rattles me.

"Adam took care of breakfast and I'll be riding with him over to the closing," I say, nodding towards Adam.

I can see Adam's jaw flex and I don't blame him. Jeremy is extra annoying today.

"Riding with him, huh? But you always ride with *me* to closings," he says, getting back to his feet.

Adam stands, watching the exchange between the both of us. I put up a hand to him, letting him know I have it.

"Jeremy, I'm going with Adam today. Please don't make a problem where there isn't one," I respond, my voice stern.

"No problem here," he says lifting his hands in defense. "I thought you were different, Genevieve. I thought you worked your way to this position respectfully."

"What the hell does that mean?" I snap.

"Making out in the elevator with Machlin Saddler and now the intern? I always respected you and your work, but now I don't know what to think," his voice laced with fake disappointment.

I flinch, remembering what he's referring to and steal a glance at Adam. His jaw is tight, his teeth clenched, and I close my eyes, exhaling.

"Jeremy, please leave my office."

"Of course."

He turns, walking towards my door and slamming it shut behind him.

"Adam...what he said about Machlin and I--"

"It's fine. Really, it's not a big deal," he says, waving his hand.

I furrow my brows and look at him, and his anger from seconds ago has disappeared.

"Don't you want to know if it's true or not?" I ask, confused.

He looks up at me, his expression surprised and then he nods.

"Right, yeah...is it true then?"

"No..." I say skeptically. "It's not true. We were in the elevator together, but nothing happened and that was before our date."

"Great. Good."

He smiles, digging into his breakfast again and I study him.

"You're a very trusting man. You believed me before I even defended myself. Why?"

"You don't seem like the type to be messing around with two men, Genevieve. I know you care for Kenzie and that would be confusing to her. I take everything Jeremy says with a grain of salt," he says with a shrug.

Before I can respond, the phone on my desk rings and I answer it.

"Saddler Enterprises, Genevieve Langston."

"Hi Genn, it's Whitney from the bank."

"Hi Whit! I thought Farrah was supposed to be on this closing today?" I ask with confusion.

"She just called and must have come down with something. I'm running a little late since it was last minute, but you guys can start without me and I'll catch up," she says out of breath.

"No worries, take your time. See you soon."

I hang up and take one last bite of my breakfast before standing.

"That was Whitney Roark. She's the bank representative today and she's running late. Let's get a jump start over there to settle things while we wait for her."

"Does that happen a lot? Bank representatives switching right before a close?" Adam asks, standing too.

"Not all the time but it does happen. Whit makes some wicked money since they always ask her. She's super sweet."

"Let me...make a phone call quick, check on my brother and I'll meet you down at the car, okay?" Adam says, kissing my cheek.

I nod and watch him leave my office, his phone in his hand. I grab my purse and walk towards my office, shutting and locking the door before walking towards the elevators. As I walk inside, Jeremy's words invade my brain again and I shake them off. I can't believe Machlin was so careless to ambush me in the elevator like that and what type of security does he have if Jeremy found out? I really hope that's not the rumor going around the office. I've worked too hard to be looked at as the office tramp. Dammit.

Chapter 10
Genevieve

I hear a knock on my door and smile shyly when Adam walks in. The past few days have been a dream with him, and I feel a tingle in my belly as he turns around, a solemn expression on his face.

"Hey, what happened?" I ask, walking around the side of my desk.

I grab his hand and drag him to sit at one of my chairs as I take the seat next to him.

"I don't know how to tell you this, Gen. I know you're going to hate me, just know none of this has to do with you. I didn't do it to hurt you, okay? You have to know that."

I clearly hear the regret in his voice and I sit back, dropping his hand into his lap while putting distance between us.

"What--" I clear my throat, ridding the hurt from my tone. "What happened?"

I watch as Adam stands, loosening his tie and he walks towards my door, locking it.

"Adam..."

I get to my feet, backing up a little, unsure of what's about to happen. He messes with something on his face and slowly turns around, without his mustache.

"What..."

He puts his fingers into his eyes, taking out contacts and then his hands are at his hair, pulling the brown mop off his head.

"M-Machlin? What is this?" I ask shocked.

"It's been me the whole time. I--"

"The whole time?!" I yell. "T-the kissing. The dates, the...that's been you?"

My voice is panicked, and I sit at my desk, my hand against my chest, slowing my heartbeat.

"It's been me, but let me explain," he says walking closer.

"Jesus Christ, I'm a fucking idiot. Why did you do this?" I snap, getting to my feet. "Embarrassing me at your house months ago wasn't enough? Ambushing me in my office, groping me in the elevator? What the fuck, Machlin? Why-- no, fuck it, I dont want to know what sick game you're playing. Get out of my office," I yell, pointing towards the door.

"Genevieve, please let me fill you in on--"

"Let me fill *you* in!" I grit through clenched teeth. "Don't you dare come near me. We've worked fine the past few months while you were away, let's just continue the way we were. I'll start looking for a new job. This is *exactly* what I was afraid of, why I don't do this! Elijah and Rochelle will give me a recommendation, please don't put your nose into that, too."

"Don't do that, Genevieve. I know you're angry, Rochelle wanted to tell you, but it was part of the plan and we couldn't--"

"Rochelle knew?" I whisper.

"She recognized me, but it's not a joke, Genevieve. Someone is stealing from the company..." he walks closer to me, but I put up my hand and he stops walking.

"Tell me you don't think it's *me*," I seethe.

"Of course not. We think it's Jeremy and since you're the only one he closes with him we--"

"Used me to get to him. God, I'm so stupid. This is why you've been trying to get into my pants? To rile him up? It's been working, you know. He's worse than ever, so thank you," I say, with a sarcastic laugh.

That's all this was. A ploy to get to Jeremy, none of it was real. I close my eyes, taking a deep breath as I feel the hope I had of possibly starting something with Adam disappear...shatter. I confided in him, I told him things I never told anyone before, and it was...Machlin.

"Get out," I whisper.

"Genevieve, you know if you were in my position you would have done the same thing. I worked my ass off, started this from nothing, and having a slimy piece of shit threaten that isn't going to fly with me. This was business, you need to understand that."

Adam is gone and in his place is Mr. Asshole CEO cold-hearted Machlin Saddler.

"Business, huh? So if we fucked in the office, in *my* office, that would have been *'just business'* too?" I snap, crossing my arms over my chest.

He lets out a low growl and closes his eyes. He moves his head, cracking his neck and then those gorgeous blue eyes lock on mine.

"I wouldn't have let it get that far," he says sternly.

I laugh and walk closer to him, slowly as my heels tap on the marble floor. I stand in front of him, running my red manicured finger down his suit jacket. Fuck him if he thinks he's not just as attracted to me as I am him. This was not "just business" and I'll be damned if he puts me in that neat little box.

"I doubt if I dropped my panties to the floor and bent over my desk, you would have denied taking every advantage of that, *Mr. Saddler*," I whisper, pulling on his tie. My lips touch his earlobe and he doesn't flinch like I hoped he would. "Now leave and patiently wait for my two weeks notice."

I let go of his tie and turn but not before he grabs my arm, turning me around and slamming my back to the door. He holds my wrists above my head against the wooden door and I struggle to break free.

"I'm still your boss, Genevieve."

"Exactly, so get the hell off me," I complain.

He presses his body hard into mine, our noses touching, his erection pressed against my belly. I let my lips form into a sly smile as I wiggle a little, eliciting a growl from his sexy mouth. Fucking asshole with a hot mouth.

"Is this still 'just business'?" I ask, arching my eyebrow.

"I will black ball you across every state in the fucking country, Genevieve Langston. You're not going anywhere. You're my best employee and no one else will take advantage of your *skills*, besides me."

"You would do that? Black ball me?" I ask dumbfounded. "You are seriously such an asshole. I have Kenzie and--"

"I'll add $100,000 to your Christmas bonus. How does that sound?"

I drop my mouth open and shake my head, struggling to comprehend his words.

"Wh-what the hell would you do that for?"

"Because we're this close to nabbing Jeremy and when we do, you're the one who deserves the money he took. You're the reason we have the evidence on him. I'm not kidding with you, Genevieve, I won't allow another company to take you."

He drops my hands and I rub at my wrists, pushing past him towards my desk.

"You don't own me, Machlin. I can do whatever I want. I *like* working here so I will stay, but so help me God, if there are any more secrets you are keeping--"

"There's not and thank you. I'll have Falon send some stuff down for you, okay?"

"So this is it then? Adam is done, huh?" I ask, letting out a breath.

"Yes, he's done after today. Our lawyer is putting everything together. Just...act normal, okay?"

He puts his mustache back on, reaching inside his suit jacket for his contact case. I watch as he puts new ones in, his wig in place, adjusting it and a pit settles in my stomach.

It wasn't the physical attraction because I now know why he looked so goofy. No, what I'll miss is the emotional one, the vulnerability Adam showed with me. How he could be sexy and sweet at the same time. Machlin is just demanding and rude. The perfect guy doesn't exist.

"I'm heading out to go upstairs and change and what not. I wasn't planning on doing it this soon. I can help you with those accounts if you--"

I put up my hand and shake my head.

"I can handle them on my own. Back to how we were, remember? I don't run into you and you go back to pretending I don't exist, at least *trying* to."

"Genevieve, the second my eyes landed on you, I would never be able to forget you existed."

With that he leaves my office, not a look back and not another word.

Chapter 11
Genevieve

I lean against the counter in the break room, sipping my coffee from the throw away cup. I have a coffee machine in my office, but I can't go in there right now; I need space. It's been three days since Adam--*Machlin*--dropped the bomb on me and I can't get past the hurt.

He was so sweet as Adam; we talked, we got to know each other, we *kissed*. He helped me tuck in Kenzie, I invited him into my home, all while he held onto this secret. God, I'm such a fool. My man radar is totally off. How the hell did I not figure this out sooner? Rochelle did, dammit. I was so blind.

"I can hear you thinking from here," says a man's voice from behind me.

I turn and see Troy, one of the contractors Rochelle uses and give him a smile.

"Hey, Troy."

"Why are you slumming it with us common folk in here?" he asks, reaching towards the K-cups.

"I...just needed to take a walk for a little."

I turn to leave but his voice stops me.

"Plans tonight? We can grab a drink or--"

"She's busy."

His voice. The commanding, no-bullshit voice that causes Troy to turn white and scurry out of the room.

"Is this the new trend now, Machlin? Stalking me?" I snap, sipping my coffee and turning towards him in the doorway.

"In my office. *Now.*"

He turns, leaving me in the break room and I roll my eyes.

"Fucking asshole," I whisper.

I finish my coffee, taking my time and toss the cup into the garbage. I walk towards my office, grab my bag, checking my appearance in my mirror and then walk to the elevators. I press the button for the top floor when my phone dings from my bag.

Machlin: What part of *now* didn't you understand, Ms. Langston?

I laugh out loud, angrily typing my reply.

Genevieve: What part of *fuck off,* don't *you* understand, Mr. Saddler?

I hover over the send button but then erase it, deciding to ignore him instead. He doesn't get to have my reaction. Screw him.

The elevator stops on the top floor and I stride out, bypassing the secretary and heading towards Rochelle's office. I've been avoiding her, hurt by her not being truthful with me, but I need my friend back. I knock quietly and hear shuffling and her muffled voice for me to enter.

I see her wiping at her eyes, and she clears her throat, looking up from her desk.

"Hey," she says, with a fake smile.

Her eyes are red, and I rush to her side, pulling her in for a hug.

"I'm sorry I've been ignoring you," I say, sniffling into her hair.

"I'm so sorry, Genn. I told him I was going to tell you, but then Jeremy and...it wasn't my place, I can't get involved. I'm sorry, though. I hated keeping that from you."

She wipes at her eyes again and I grip her shoulders.

"I hope all this isn't because of me," I say, motioning to her sad expression.

She waves a hand away and lets out a practiced laugh.

"I'm fine, really. Can we do taco night tonight?" she asks with hope.

"Of course. If I don't end up in jail from murdering your brother, then sure," I say, rolling my eyes. "I'm headed there now but I couldn't walk past without seeing you, putting the shit behind us. I've missed you," I say, hugging her again.

"I've missed you, too. Please don't ever do this again. My brother is a dick, don't punish me for his crimes. They'll be a lot, believe me," she groans.

"Well if you hear a commotion, please come and save me from a lifetime of orange jumpsuits."

She laughs and hugs me again, pushing me towards the door.

I walk down the hall towards Machlin's office and open the door without knocking. He's standing, his back to me, looking out the floor to ceiling window that overlooks the city.

"Shut the door," he snaps.

I roll my eyes and shut the door, the loud click echoing off the walls.

"Have you slept with him?" Machlin asks.

"Who?" I ask confused.

He turns around, his hands in his suit pockets and his stare is deadly--cold.

"The prick that was trying to get you to go out with him downstairs."

I laugh and shake my head. "Troy? No, I have not slept with Troy and I don't plan on it. Not all men want to sleep with me, Machlin. He's a friend and it's really not any of your business!" I shout.

"Good, because you're going to be working under me now," he says, his voice hard and demanding.

"Oh, am I?" I cross my arms over my chest and arch an eyebrow. "What if I work better on top?"

I see his Adam's Apple bob and he lets out a slow groan, his nostrils flaring. He can tell me how the chemistry between Adam and me--*Machlin* and me--was just for the job, but he's a shit liar. I saw it in my office, and I see it again now.

"Don't push me, Genevieve."

"I'm not, *Machlin*."

"If we're going to work together--"

"I thought I said I'll go back to what I was doing, and you'll go back to whatever it is *you* do. How did you translate that to me wanting to work with you?" I scoff.

"You're amazing at sales, staging houses, and gaining clients trust. I have never seen anything like that aside from myself."

"Incredibly humble of you," I mumble.

"I want to work with you, teach you everything I know. We could make Saddler Enterprises even bigger than I've ever imagined. You once told me that you've followed me, wanted to pick my brain. Does that offer still stand?"

"Oh, the day you got me drunk and took advantage of me, just to prove you could?"

"We need to forget the past."

"Forget what? The kiss with Mr. Fake Intern Adam? Or the kiss with the almighty Machlin Saddler? I'm losing track of the many men I've kissed, oh wait, it's just been one!"

"Exactly! Stop going around kissing every man you meet!"

I gasp and clutch my chest, letting out a cynical laugh.

"I cannot believe you just said that!"

"Genny..."

"Don't Genny, me. Adam knew me like that, not you!"

"I was Adam!"

"No, you weren't, you were pretending to be! I would have never confided in this cold, calculating man like I did him," I say, poking his chest.

He grabs my finger and pulls me to him, our bodies pressed together.

"Maybe that *was* me. Maybe I'm really not that big of a dick."

He pushes a strand of hair out of my eyes and I close them, hating myself for loving his touch, believing his words.

"We shouldn't do this though," he says, quickly backing away from me.

My eyes snap open and I furrow my brows.

"God, you're more irritating than I could have ever imagined." I stomp towards the door. "Kiss my ass, Machlin."

"I'm pretty sure if you bent forward just the slightest, I could. Maybe you should wear something more professional tomorrow, Ms. Langston. It could be distracting to the rest of the employees."

His tone is harsh, and I grit my teeth, turning back slowly.

"Not that big of a dick, my ass. Distracting to other employees or just you?"

He arches an eyebrow at my tone, and I cross my arms over my chest. Apparently, this is my signature stance around this infuriating man.

"I would prefer if you didn't use dick and ass in the same sentence either, unless it's a request," he smirks.

"I swear, you..." I take a deep breath and know he's waiting for a reaction. Nope. Not giving it to him. "Fine," I retort. "Have a great day, *Mr. Saddler.*"

I slam his office door shut and let out a frustrated breath as I walk back to my own. He wants a more modest attire he's got another thing coming.

Machlin

"What did you do to Gen?" my sister Rochelle asks the next morning, as she comes into my office.

"Nothing. She's still pissed about my undercover boss routine and I told her she answers to me now. It's for her own benefit, really. She'll learn a lot underneath me."

She lets out a sarcastic laugh and drops to the chair in front of my desk.

"Oh, I'm sure she will," she smirks. "Anyways, was any part of that speech, 'I"ll fuck you on my desk today?' Because she looks like sex on a stick. I'm seriously debating on adding a female section to my fuckadex."

"Your what?" I ask, before waving my hand away. "Never mind, I don't want to know. What do you mean, 'sex on a stick'? I told her tone it down, dammit."

"You did not," Rochelle groans. "Seriously, Mac? You can't tell a woman to do that, what's wrong with you? Especially Gen! You can't pretend you didn't know she'd do the *opposite* of what you said!"

"Well, I hoped she wouldn't, I'm still her boss!" I snap.

"Sometimes we can't always get what we hope for," says a sexy voice from the doorway. "For example, I wanted to take a chance and date my charming, perfect intern but little did I know, he was a wolf in sheep's clothing."

I look up and close my eyes, cursing my big mouth for telling Genevieve to dress less sexy. There she stands in my doorway with a red, lace dress, her curves suffocating, beautiful tits on display as she saunters into the room, sitting at the chair next to Rochelle.

"Yeah, I'm going. I'll lock the door on my way out," Rochelle laughs as she gets to her feet.

I hear the door shut and lock, filling the silence in the room. I can't open my eyes, I keep them shut, trying to get myself under control.

"We're working blindfolded today, huh? Never done that before, but I'm game," she says, her voice dripping with seduction.

I snap my eyes open and zero in on her, leaned back in the chair, hands folded over her stomach. She's tapping her fingers with her legs crossed, a sassy shit eating grin on her face.

"I see you follow orders well. That how you managed to work your way up so fast?"

Her smile drops and she stops tapping her finger. She gives me that look. The look of hatred and it suddenly fills my body with a calm I only seem to get from her. Why do her reactions do this to me?

"Are you insinuating I *fucked* my way to the top *again*, Mr. Saddler?"

I groan at her words and get to my feet quickly, moving to stand in front of her but she doesn't move a muscle. Her hard gaze is still burning a hole in me, making me hard.

"I sure as shit hope you didn't. No one at this company will *fuck* you except me."

I lean forward, my hands on the arm rests, caging her body against the chair.

121

She slowly sits up, her expression stone as she uncrosses her legs and reaches for my tie. She pulls on it so her red lips press against my ear.

"Let me make this clear, Mr. Saddler. *I* will fuck *you*. Long gone is the lost woman that walked into this building on her first day and the fangirl from dinner, so keep your fucking hands to yourself until I tell you otherwise."

She kisses the side of my neck as I shiver, itching to touch her but respecting her words. I take a breath, her perfume--raspberry and blackberries--filling my nostrils.

I reluctantly step back as she slowly stands, her body moving against mine as she gets to her feet. Our faces are inches away; I could kiss her, wrap her in my arms and make her beg for my touch, for a fuck against my desk, but I refrain.

I lick my lips, watching her eyes darken at the movement. She can act like she's in control, but she has absolutely none.

"I'll be in my office if you need anything today. Of course I'm at your service, Mr. Saddler."

She lifts her hooded eyes to mine, and I smirk, knowing that it won't be long until she weakens, until we both weaken to what we want. She turns to leave and because I'm the bastard that I am, I press her a little harder wanting more reaction from her, more hatred.

"Thanks for the hard work, Genevieve." I grab a handful of her ass and she stops walking.

"Grab my ass again and I'll break every single one of your fingers, *Mr. Saddler.*"

She turns without slapping me right across my face and I watch as her ass sways out of my office. I adjust myself in my dress pants with a smile.

She is right though, the women from the plane is long gone. She was lost and hurt--fragile. This woman though, this woman is strong, cold and confident. She won't fall as easily to me but I'm Machlin again and Machlin Saddler never backs down from a challenge.

Your body is mine, Genevieve.

Chapter 12
Machlin

I pull my Benz up to the iron gate of the house Gen and I are supposed to be staging and type in the code. Normally, I would let her work on her own, but the past few days she's pushed my fucking buttons like no one has before.

I want her and for some reason she won't break in the office. So, here I am today, outside of the office trying to get her to crumble to me. It's a sick addiction I have, her dislike of me, her revulsion. When I spar with her, I think of nothing else, only the adrenaline coursing through my body, giving me a twisted feeling of relaxation. I know it would be even stronger when we finally fuck and I want to feel that, even just for a second.

I park my car on the side and my dick almost hits the steering wheel as she walks out of the house to the company truck to unload more furniture. How could I forget what her staging outfit did to me?

I see those sexy legs move as they make their way to my side door and she taps on my window, hands on her hips.

I roll it down, pushing my sunglasses up to my head and smile at her.

"Morning, sunshine. How are you on this lovely Tuesday?"

"What the hell are you doing here, Machlin?"

"Helping you stage," I say, rolling up my window and opening my car door.

I stand, wrapping an arm around Genevieve's waist and turn her, pushing her back into my car. She squeals and I press my body hard into hers.

"You didn't think I'd miss an opportunity to see these gorgeous bare legs and imagine them wrapped around my waist, did you?" I whisper, trailing a finger up her thigh and underneath the hem of her shorts.

She sucks in a breath and pushes me off.

"I don't need you to help me stage. I've been doing it for years, thank you very much."

She stomps towards the truck to grab a side table and I jog after her, grabbing a lamp before it crashes to the ground.

"Let me at least bring everything in then. You can put it where it belongs. I won't get in the way, but I'll offer suggestions if they're needed. Deal?"

"Fine," she reluctantly agrees.

She leaves the table in the truck and turns on her heel, walking back into the house. I grin, shaking my head as I bring in the coffee table and lamp and set them down in the foyer.

I hear a commotion in the kitchen and follow the sound, seeing Genevieve hanging pots from the rack above the island stove top, that fucking tattoo mocking me.

I come up behind her, grabbing a pot that she's struggling to hook and let my hand run down her side, grazing her ribs slightly and to her hip. I rest my other hand on the counter next to her body, caging her in.

"We both want this, Genevieve. Let's finally acknowledge this chemistry so we can move on, no?" I whisper, brushing her stray hairs away from the back of her neck, kissing it.

Her skin is soft under my lips and I breathe in her scent. The scent I've craved every day I walked into her office as her intern, hell even on that damn plane.

"I thought you said it was for the job," she pants, grabbing the back of my neck and massaging a knot that's formed.

"The feelings were, yes, but any warm-blooded man would want you, Genevieve. I'm no different."

I run my hand down her belly and snap open her jean shorts, moving my hand down slowly, waiting for her to stop me, but she doesn't.

I inch it down more, slipping inside her panties and fuck she's bare. A shaved, wet pussy for me and I swear I want to just slam my cock right inside her, bare and rough, cracking this fucking counter.

"Jesus Christ," I groan, through my gritted teeth. "Don't stop me, Genevieve. Please don't fucking stop me."

"Beg me not to," she whispers.

I move my hand against her clit, and she lets out a loud moan, dropping her head back to my shoulder.

"Oh God, it's been so long," she murmurs, breathlessly.

"Come all over my fingers, Genevieve."

I move my thumb faster against her clit and then slip a finger inside her, as far as it can go and then another one. Her walls suffocate my fingers, stretching so good for me.

"Mmmm, I want to taste you," I whisper, pulling my fingers out and bringing them to my lips.

I lick them clean as I see Genevieve watching from the corner of her eye, sinking her teeth into her bottom lip, whimpering.

"You want a taste?" I grin.

She nods silently as I slip my fingers into her mouth and she sucks as I push my erection harder into her ass.

"You want my mouth around your cock like this?" she sasses, as she sucks my fingers harder.

"You want me to fucking destroy you? Tear this pussy to shreds and ruin it for any man after me?"

I bite the lobe of her ear hard and she gasps, gritting her teeth.

"Finish what you started. Don't be a disappointment, Machlin."

"I *always* finish what I start, *sweetheart*."

I push my body harder into her, pushing my hand against her pussy. She jumps at the pressure and I wrap my other arm around her front, pinching her nipple through her tank top. She bucks against me, gripping the counter as she starts to shake, her slick walls gripping my fingers.

"Yesss, so close," she moans.

I work my fingers faster, pumping them in and out of her, crooking them against her g-spot and then she's there, screaming my name as she leans back, exposing her neck to me. I latch onto it, sucking and biting as she groans with satisfaction and I growl in her ear.

"Tell me to keep going," I plead.

"Are you begging me to?" she whispers with a smile, turning to face me.

She trails a finger down the front of my t-shirt to the tent in my shorts and I slam my hands down on both sides of her, closing my eyes.

"Just...repay the favor, baby."

"Beg. Me. To," she stresses, enunciating every word as her nail runs along my shaft through my shorts.

Shit, that feels so good. Why can't I just say it, dammit? She squeezes my length through my shorts and moves her hand down, finding my balls and squeezing those too. I want her skin on my skin, I *need* her skin on my skin.

"I want this, Genevieve. You can clearly see I do just--"

"I want to hear you say it wasn't just because of Jeremy. I want to hear you say you've wanted me since you met me. It wasn't just some bullshit for the case and we both know it. Say it and I'll drop to my knees right here and swallow your cock and let you come down my throat."

Her voice is desperate, needy and hoarse and I wonder if I could make her break without having to admit that she's right. Fuck, she's right. I looked forward to spending the day with her, kissing her, talking with her. Tucking Kenzie into bed with her felt *right*, cuddling on the couch felt...*normal*. Fuck. Fuck. Fuck. She doesn't need this shit, what am I doing?

I back away from her, running my hand through my hair and walk back outside towards the company truck. I grab another table, prepared to bring everything inside and leave but Genevieve is standing in the doorway with her arms folded.

"You're such a fucking coward," she snaps with an angry laugh, walking closer to me. "You want this to just be a fuck, then fine, take it. I don't need a boy in my life, I need a *man*. Let's get this over with."

She puts her hand on the back of my neck and pulls my face towards hers. Our lips finally crash together, and I drop the table in between us, lifting her, quickly.

I walk back towards the front door with her legs wrapped around my waist as I lean her into the door frame because I'm a weak shit that can't control this. She groans when her back slams, but my lips attack hers again, feasting on her, remembering every fucking sound she makes, remembering every flavor coming off her tongue as it tangles with mine.

Her hand slips under the hem of my t-shirt as she runs her nails down my back, the burn from the friction making me slam my body harder into her.

"Yessss, Mac."

She starts to move on top of me, with her open shorts, using her thighs to slide up and down against my shaft. Our kiss is messy, hungry and wild as we dry hump each other against the fucking door frame of the house we're supposed be staging. Fuck professional. We've crossed that line a long damn time ago and I pull down the front of her tank top, her full breast spilling out. I suck in a breath, not prepared for this luscious tit to look so appetizing and then I feast, like a famished wolf, biting and sucking every inch of her breast.

"Holy shit, Machlin. I..."

The voice in the back of my head breaks free, telling me to keep going. Use her to get a reprieve from your grief, your problems. Keep going because it's working...the stress slowly slipping out of my body, but I can't. I'm a fucking idiot if I think burying myself into Genevieve is going to stop me from wanting to do it again...and again...and again. She shuts all the bad shit off in my life when I'm with her, fighting her, kissing her, making her come. I try to ignore the doubt, but I can't. I can't do this to her. I pull back, slowly putting her back on her feet and she shakes her head, smiling.

"You can't do it, can you?" she breathes heavily, wiping at her mouth. "You're a piece of work, Machlin Saddler. I got it from here, just go...fuck yourself."

She turns to walk back in the house and slams the door in my face. I hear the lock and turn, rubbing a hand down my face. I smile, an aggravated smile and shake my head. *You're so fucked, Machlin. So, so fucked.*

Chapter 13
Machlin

I glance up from my desk and see Genevieve striding in, her expression exhausted and she yawns, her hand covering her mouth.

"You okay?" I ask.

"Fine. What do you need me to do today? I have the Dillons scheduled to look at two of Rochelle's properties but aside from that, I'm all yours."

Her tone isn't playful or sarcastic like it normally is, it's tired.

"Why don't you take the day off? You don't look good," I press.

"I said I'm fine," she snaps. "I just need more coffee."

"Fine," I snap back. God, she's so aggravating. "I have a brunch meeting scheduled with William Donovan. Want to come?"

"When did we snag William Donovan?" she asks, sitting in the chair across from my desk.

"We didn't. Want to prove your worth?" I smirk.

"Funny. I thought that's what I've been doing," she says, rolling her eyes. "I definitely need more coffee for this then, I'll meet you down in the lobby in an hour."

I nod as she gets back to her feet and walks out the door. She's sick, or tired or maybe just sick and tired of me. I run my hands down my face, hating that I want to run out of my fucking office and hug her. Ask her what is really going on and then fix it. Adam would have done that. I'm not Adam. I could be, though. It really wasn't all that bad.

I glance down at my desk and see seven smiling faces back at me. The last picture our family took the Christmas before my parents passed away. This is what I need to be focusing on.

An hour later, I'm walking towards the lobby and see Kenzie sitting on the benches outside the childcare room, crying with Marie.

"Hey, cutie, what's the matter?" I ask, sitting down on the other side of her.

"She had a nightmare during nap time today. Genevieve said she hasn't been sleeping well."

I nod, now putting the pieces together.

"I got it. I'll bring her inside when we're done talking," I say dismissing Marie.

She nods, getting to her feet and walks back into the childcare center.

"Can I tell you a secret? Do you remember me from the plane?" I whisper with a smile. "I gave you a lolipop, remember?"

Kenzie looks up and smiles at me, rubbing her little hand along my chin. She's so fucking smart and observant already.

"I shaved," I smirk.

She takes her hand off, looking down at her feet and I tip her chin up to look at me.

"What's going on cutie? You scared?" I ask in a soft voice.

She shakes her head and I see a tear fall down her cheek. I brush it away and try to keep myself together. Fuck, I can't see this little girl cry. My cold, dead heart can't take this. It's like a defibrillator, trying to restart it.

"Miss Mama," she whispers, crying a little harder.

Boom! There it is. No shock advised. Organized rhythm.

I cradle her to my chest as she soaks my suit jacket and I let her. I know what this feels like; to have the person you care the most about ripped away from you. It sucks, it really fucking sucks.

"It's okay, cutie. You have Genny. She loves you so much."

I kiss the top of her head and she turns into me, climbing on top of my lap and wrapping her little arms around my neck. I squeeze my eyes shut and try to give her some of my strength, not that I have much left. Little Mackenzie is draining my tough exterior and I wrap my arms around her in a tighter hug.

"Kenzie! What happened?" Genevieve asks, rushing over to us.

Kenzie turns in my arms and lifts her hands up, motioning for Genn. She grabs Kenzie, pulling her to her body, soothing her.

"Shhh, it's okay baby, it's okay."

Genn runs her hand up and down Kenzie's back, playing with her little ponytail and I stand.

"Marie said she had a bad D-R-E-A-M. I asked her and she said she missed "M-O-M," I spell.

Genevieve's eyes close and she exhales. She moves her lips towards Kenzie ear and whispers something. Kenzie lifts her head up, looking at Genevieve with a big smile and nods, hugging her tightly again.

"Man too?" Kenzie asks, as she points to me.

Genevieve glances towards me and gives Kenzie a strained smile.

"He's probably busy, baby."

"Busy for what?" I ask.

"I told Kenzie we could do Disney Princess movie night. She loves Beauty and the Beast."

I let out a nervous laugh and rub the back of my neck.

"I uh...do have a lot of work. I'm not sure I can--"

Kenzie looks up at me, stopping my excuse dead in its tracks. Her sad eyes call to me. Remembering those sad, lost eyes on the faces of my younger sisters, when I had to tell them they would never see their parents again. Needing to make them feel better--say or do anything--just to get them smiling again. I close my eyes letting out a breath, knowing I feel the same pull towards Kenzie.

"Ya know what? I love Beauty and the Beast. I'm in," I say with a smile.

Kenzie smiles and Genevieve's mouth opens a few times before she speaks.

"Y-you really don't have to. She'll forget about it once the movie starts, I'm not sure this...is a good idea."

I smile, walking closer to her, bending down to whisper in her ear. Like every single time around Genevieve Langston, I need her attention to fuel me.

"Afraid you'll end up with your legs spread on your counter again? Or worse, upstairs on your back in your bed?"

She sucks in a breath and just like that, flustered Genevieve is gone and in her place is the bold badass that will tell me to shove my words down my throat. She grits her teeth and I smile, waving to Kenzie as I walk backwards to the front lobby.

"I'll be waiting in the car out front. Bye, Kenzie! See you tonight, cutie!"

I turn and smile, knowing I got Genevieve all riled up. Why does making her crazy appeal to me so much? It's fun as fuck watching her eyes turn stormy.

Thinking about tonight and heading to her house for the sole purpose of spending time with Kenzie scares the shit out of me, though. Last time, it was a "date" and I was Adam, not Machlin. Kenzie was in bed by the time I got there but this is different. I push down the feelings it stirs in me and watch the lobby door from the back of my car. I've perfected pushing my own feelings aside these past five years.

Genevieve emerges a few minutes later, the fire in her eyes still there, but I still see the exhaustion. I get out, walking around to open the back door for her and she eyes me, shaking her head. I smile, closing the door behind her and walk around to get into the backseat with her.

"Carlton Bistro, Michael," I say to my driver.

"Yes, sir."

He rolls up the partition between the back and front and I turn towards Gen.

"Is that why you look like shit? She hasn't been sleeping?"

"Ha! Thank you for that. Just what I like to hear!" she laughs sarcastically.

"You know what I mean, I--"

"Yes, that and my mother are the reasons I look like *shit.* She misses Tonya, and I don't blame her, I do too. This is so hard. I don't know if I'm doing this right. I mean I helped raise her, but it's different now. Tonya always had that...instinct that all moms have. I just--could use my mother's advice but she's...never mind, you don't wanna hear this. So, what do I need to know about William?"

I put my hand on her thigh and we both look down at the contact.

"I need my best employee to be at the top of her game so if there is something I can do to help, that's what I'm going to do. Tell me, Genevieve, what do you need from me to make this better?"

She arches an eyebrow and takes my hand off her thigh.

"Not a fuck in the back of your car if that's where this was headed. Just forget it, I'll figure it out. Back to William."

I shake my head, letting out a loud groan.

"Fine, fuck it. You're as stubborn as they come. Here's the file on William." I toss it to her with more force than I intended.

She catches it, rolling her eyes and hell if I don't want to spank the ever living shit out of her. Her mouth, her attitude, drives me absolutely out of my goddamn mind.

"Stop staring at me, it's creepy as fuck."

I let out a sarcastic laugh and lean forward so our noses are practically touching.

"You miss the comfort of Adam, so I try to give it to you. You dismiss it, so I give you *me*. You piss on that too, so I'm at a loss here, Genny."

"I miss the charm and vulnerability of Adam and...Don't. Call. Me. Genny," she says through gritted teeth.

I close my eyes, gritting my own teeth before opening them again.

"Mark my words, *Genevieve,* that when I have you on all fours on my bed, I will punish this fucking body for all the sass you have slung my way. You won't walk for days. You won't even be able to swallow your own saliva because your throat will be so raw from swallowing my cock for hours on fucking end. How's that for charming and vulnerable?"

"You're a fucking asshole."

"Again with the requests. We'll work up to that, baby."

I smirk when she lets out another sarcastic laugh and goes back to looking through the folder. A few minutes later the car comes to a stop in front of the Bistro. Genevieve waits for me to walk around and open her door, slinging a hateful glance my way and surprisingly laces her arm through mine when I extend it for her.

We walk towards the back room, William already waiting at a table for us.

"Machlin Saddler, what arm candy," he smirks, eyeing Genevieve from head to toe.

I tighten my grip on her and try and return his smile.

"My best associate broker, Ms. Genevieve Langston."

"Pleasure to meet you, Mr. Donovan," Genevieve says in her business tone, extending her hand towards William.

William takes it, arching an eyebrow and then kisses the top with a smirk.

"*Pleasure* is all mine, Ms. Langston. I am a giver with the right woman, though."

Genevieve clears her throat as she pulls her hand back and I motion for us to sit.

"So, William. We've obtained land for three types of projects I think you'll be very interested in," I say, taking a sip from my water.

I motion towards Genevieve and she leans forward, putting her hands on the table.

"We have a luxury apartment-Galleria blueprint in the works. Five retail stores, one coffee shop, and one upscale Mediterranean restaurant which our analytical team thinks--"

"I'm sorry," William says interrupting her, waving his hand. "I can't talk business without a drink in my hand. Your beauty is just...distracting."

He smiles, motioning to our waiter and orders a bottle of the most expensive wine on the menu. I ball my fists at the side but try to keep my composure.

"William, Genevieve is more than just a pretty face. She's been working on this project the last month and it would be a great asset to your portfolio. If you're not interested in more than just getting into my associate's panties, then I'm afraid we have to cut this meeting short."

I don't care if I sound like an asshole--I *am* an asshole.

"Working very hard on this indeed," William says, arching an eyebrow between the two of us. "Sharing is caring, Machlin. Let me see how *hard* Ms. Langston really works and then I'll give you my answer, deal?"

I hear Genevieve scoff from next to me.

"I am not some cheap--"

I put a hand up, dismissing her words and lean forward across the table, making sure William sees my death stare for what it is--a threat. The only person that talks to Genevieve that way is me, dammit.

"I don't think you heard me right, William. *We* don't need *you* on this project, *you* need *us*. It's being built with or without you. It would benefit everyone, of course, but there are plenty of you out there. Genevieve Langston is a Saddler Enterprises employee and when my employees aren't happy, neither am I. This brunch is over, and if you ever decide to do business with us again--lose my fucking card, because I sure as *fuck* am not goning to be on board."

I stand, holding my hand out to Genevieve and she takes it as I wrap her arm with mine. We walk briskly out to my waiting car and she stops on the sidewalk, whipping around and grabbing my tie.

"Don't make the mistake of thinking I'll fall to my knees at your feet for what you did," she snaps. "You're still that arrogant son of a bitch that took advantage of me."

I smirk, wrapping my hand around hers, moving my face closer.

"Don't be surprised if I fall to mine. Your hatred for me is the biggest turn on of all."

She scoffs and pulls her hand away, walking to the car. I open her door, watching as she slides inside.

"I could have handled that myself, ya know?" she says, trying to make her voice hard, but it's not. It's fatigued, overworked and exhausted.

"I know you could have but I protect my employees, Genevieve. What he was suggesting--"

"Employees, huh? None of that had to do with the raw jealousy written all over your face?"

I hear amusement in her tone and grit my teeth. Business. This was supposed to be a business meeting and I need to remember that. I can't just act on emotion and fuck if Genevieve isn't right. I was jealous and I wanted to rip William's head off for even suggesting I let him "work" Genevieve. What a fucking scumbag.

"I'll drop you at the office, I have other shit to attend to."

I don't look at her, continuing to stare at the window so I miss her reaction. I can probably guess it was an eyeroll or her folding her arms across her chest, though. I wait a few minutes and quickly steal a glance sideways and sure enough, her arms are folded, shaking her head as her lips move.

"What was that? I can't really hear you?" I say.

"Nothing, I'm talking to myself."

"Anything good?"

"For you, sure. Trying to talk myself out of murdering you."

I choke on a laugh as she turns back towards the window, still shaking her head. I sigh, letting my head drop to the headrest as we take the rest of the ride in silence.

When we pull up to my building I get out, opening Genevieve's door and she starts to walk away. I grab her wrist and turn her around.

"What time tonight?" I ask.

"Let's just...rain check, okay?"

She pulls her wrist out of my hand and walks inside without a look back. I know William's words hurt her. She doesn't like to seem weak, so she runs and I don't blame her, I'm the same. I shake my head and walk back towards the car getting in the back seat.

"Where to, sir?"

"Is there some place to get candy and junk food around here?" I ask.

"Yes, sir."

Chapter 14
Genevieve

I walk right into my mother's house because apparently, she doesn't even lock the door now.

"Mama?" I call through the hall.

The house is dark and I start to panic, walking quickly down the hall to her bedroom. I burst the door open and see her flinch from her chair by the window. I sigh, putting my hand over my chest and feel the relief flood my body.

"Mama, you left the door unlocked. You really should--"

"I don't care, Genevieve. I don't care about anything anymore."

I stand in my spot, frozen at her words. She's barely said two words to me the past month and those are the one's she chooses to say?

"Mama, you still have me," I whisper, walking towards her.

"You look so much like him," she says softly, turning her face to look at me. "I always loved that about you, but now it breaks my heart."

I see the pain in her eyes, and it tears me to pieces that I can't help her, that I'm not enough to pull her out of this. If anything, I make it worse.

"Mama, please let me get someone to help you. I miss him too, so, so much. He wouldn't want us to live like this, he would want us to stay together and be happy and--"

"I can't be happy, Genevieve! Don't you see? Your father is gone! The love of my life was ripped away from me for no goddamn good reason!"

I flinch at her words and she lets out a breath, looking towards the window again.

"Mama, I'm here. I'm your daughter. That doesn't count for anything? I lost him, too, dammit! He was my father!" My anger rises at her selfishness, my inability to stop her from hurting.

I don't even know who I'm angrier at; her or myself.

"I'm sorry, Mama. I shouldn't have raised my voice like that, I just--"

She puts up her hand to stop me and shakes her head.

"Please let me be, Genevieve. Please just let me be."

I get to my feet and look at her, waiting for her to tell me she is just hurt and angry and she didn't mean it, but she doesn't. I stand there in silence, staring at her as she looks out the window, unaffected.

I silently nod and walk out of the room and out of the front door, locking it behind me. I get to my car and once I'm inside, I break down, shedding tears for my father, for my mother and myself. Taking care of Kenzie, making sure my mother doesn't do anything to harm herself, keeping up with things at work; it's all like a weight over my head that's ready to drop down at any second. I cry until there is nothing left in my body and then drive back to work to finish my day and pick up Kenzie.

I walk into the living room with the popcorn and bag of Twizzlers as Kenzie jumps around the couch, giggling.

"Sit down, crazy girl! You'll get a boo-boo."

She plops down on her butt and the doorbell rings.

"Auntie Elle is here!" I say excitedly.

I put the food down on the coffee table and walk towards the front door, nearly fainting when I take a good look at what is in front of me.

Machlin in a t-shirt, shorts and a backwards Arizona Diamondbacks hat. Holy hell, I thought the suit wearing Machlin was delicious, but this "comfy" Machlin may have him beat.

"W-what are you doing here? I thought we agreed--"

"*You* agreed." He pushes past me into my house. "I didn't agree to shit."

"But Rochelle is--"

"Sick. Poor thing."

He smiles as Kenzie runs up to him, jumping into his body.

"Hi, Man!"

"Hi, cutie," he says back.

"Machlin, how did you even...ya know what? Forget it. Fine, you win. We were just about to start the movie."

He nods, lifting Kenzie and hands me a plastic bag.

"I uh...wasn't sure what to get. The lady at the store helped me."

His uncharacteristic uncertainty is so disarming. A glimpse of Adam flashes in my mind, but I push it away. He was pretending, Genn. Pre-tend-ing!

"Right, well I made popcorn. Do you want a beer or wine or something?"

"What are you drinking?" he asks.

"Water."

"Good thing I brought over some beers then," he says winking.

He walks past me into the living room, holding Kenzie like it's the most natural thing in the world.

I walk to the kitchen to take a breath and compose myself before I let my heart--or my vagina--shut off my brain. I'm an emotional disaster today; between the meeting this morning and then seeing my mother. My body can't be trusted to make good decisions tonight. It'll use Machlin to shut it off just like it always tries to do.

"Get it together, Genevieve. It's Machlin fucking Saddler. Machlin *asshole* Saddler!"

I finally feel strong enough, so I walk into the living room and for the second time tonight, Machlin knocks me right on my ass.

"Beeeee ourrrrrr guest, be our guest, put our service to the test!"

Machlin sings on the top of his lungs as he twirls Kenzie around in her Belle nightgown. I lean against the door frame, my hand over my chest and fight so hard to push down these feelings; feelings other than hate for Machlin.

"Fun, Man!" Kenzie yells, as she collapses to the couch.

Machlin laughs, a full-on belly chuckle as he catches his breath. The sound wraps itself around my heart and squeezes so fucking hard, I have no choice but to feel it.

Shit.

I clear my throat and walk further in, sitting on the couch next to Kenzie.

"You a big Disney buff?" I ask with a smile.

His smile slowly fades, and he nods a sad nod.

"I'm sure you know my parents passed away."

I nod silently, kicking myself for not putting all these pieces together.

"Having three younger sisters to take care of will kind of force info into your brain you really don't want there," he laughs wryly. "Like the words to every damn Disney song."

I laugh too as we both lock eyes. There's something different in his gaze tonight, something...vulnerable and as quickly as it came, it's gone. He blinks and turns away, reaching for the bag, taking out a beer and handing me one.

"Cheers," he says with a fake smile, clinking our cans together.

"Cheers."

I turn and start the movie as Kenzie cuddles up in between us, leaning her head against Machlin's ribs and putting her feet in my lap. I subconsciously rub her legs and see Machlin running his fingers through her hair out of the corner of my eyes.

This feels too right. Cuddling on the couch, watching a Disney movie with Kenzie and Machlin, like a...*family*. All of my worries are suddenly disappearing, and I want them to...I want this to last.

Shit, again.

I turn and focus back on the movie, and a little while later I hear quiet snores coming from Kenzie's little nose.

"At least she made it halfway," Machlin smirks. "Want me to carry her to bed?"

"I--" I clear my throat and start again. "I can do it."

I gently lift Kenzie in my arms as she sleepily opens her eyes and looks at Machlin.

"Night, Man," she says with a yawn, blowing Machlin a kiss.

"Night, princess," he replies softly, leaning up to kiss her on the forehead.

I see her smile, shut her eyes and bury her face into my chest, and I'm done for. I'm so, so done for. Machlin Saddler *does* have a soft side and it is going to be my downfall. Just for tonight though, I am going to capitalize on it. I need the distraction, I need the feeling of everything being right in the world, even if it's just for tonight.

Machlin

I stand from the couch, rubbing my hand down my face and pace around the living room floor. I should leave. I need to get the fuck out of here because this is too real, too...serious. I finish my can of beer and walk to the kitchen, putting it in the sink.

"Fucking hell, Mac. What the fuck have you done?" I whisper to myself.

Why can't I have this? Why can't I enjoy this? What the hell is wrong with me? Why can't I be there for my family, but also have one of my own? I don't know what to do with these...*feelings.* I shudder at the realization that I have *feelings* for someone. This shouldn't make me panic, I've always wanted this. Then my parents died and all of that died with them.

"You heading out already?" I hear a soft voice say from the doorway.

I jump, Genevieve's soothing tone breaking me out of my negative thoughts. I turn and look at her and only now realize what she's wearing. Short as hell pajama shorts and a skin-tight tank top, leaving nothing to my imagination. I see her nipples poking through the thin material and groan.

I eye her as she walks towards me, her steps determined until she stops in front of me, running her nail down the front of my t-shirt to the waistband of my shorts.

"I like this casual wardrobe, Mr. Saddler," she smirks.

I lift my lips in a cocky smile because I need my defenses in place. I need to remind myself that Genevieve Langston deserves a man like Adam, not like me.

"And I like yours, although I'd prefer naked."

I expect her to slap me, but this is my equal, she gives it right back to me instead.

"So then stop undressing me with your eyes and start doing it with your teeth, *boss*."

I groan, cupping her cheek. I'm a fucking mess over here, wanting to push her away but then pulling her back to bury my cock inside her. I remember her today though, exhausted and defeated. Asshole William, Kenzie not sleeping, things not going well with her mother. She's using me tonight, I can see it in her eyes.

"These games are frustrating, Genevieve."

"You're making it a game, Machlin. I just want you to admit the truth we both know. I'll only wait so long before I find what I want with you, from someone else," she says with frustration.

I don't blame her. I fingered her against the fucking counter the other day, almost take her against the door frame and now, here we are all alone in her house and I'm thinking of fucking leaving. Cat and mouse, mouse and cat. I don't even know which one I am anymore.

I see her studying me, looking for any indication of where my head is at, but even I don't have a fucking clue. She doesn't deserve to be riled up and left unsatisfied though-- that I do know--and bringing her to a release will bring me one too.

"Take off your shorts," I murmur, flicking her hard nipple through her tank top.

She flinches and jumps as I spin her around and push her back to the wall.

"W-what do you mean ta--"

149

"Take. Off. Your. Fucking. Shorts. I *am* speaking English, Genevieve."

Her eyebrows furrow and she smacks my hand off her breast.

"Don't talk to me like I--"

I cut her off with a kiss and untie her short strings in one smooth motion, grabbing her hands that are trying to push me off her. I pin them above her head against the wall and break the kiss, studying her. She's panting, her plump breasts heaving up and down and I dip my head down, sucking on the delicious meat there.

"Oh God," she moans.

"I'm letting go of your wrists to drop down to my knees and eat you until you pass out on my face. Can you just accept that and not fight me? Because if you can't I can easily do it with your hands restrained behind your back," I growl.

She furrows her brows again, her lips forming into a tight line, stopping her from lashing out at me like I know she wants to.

"I...want to touch you," she admits, trying to free her wrists.

"And I want you to touch me, but only if you're going to push my face harder into your pussy. Don't pull me off or so help me God, Genevieve Langston, I will restrain every limb you have and devour your body until you're crying and begging for mercy. I want to make you feel good, I want to have your taste on my tongue the rest of the night. Can you handle that? Can you for once do what you're fucking told?"

I let go of her wrists as she nods, crossing her arms over her chest in a defiant pose.

"I've never been so angry at a man that offered to eat me out before. Why are you so goddamn frustrating, Machlin Saddler?"

I drop to my knees, pulling her shorts and thong down in one motion and slam her body harder into the wall. I lift her leg up over my shoulder and smile as she gasps.

"Just shut up, Genny."

I launch my face forward and consume every fucking inch of her sweet pussy. For months I've dreamt of her taste, daydreamed about the sounds she would make as I assaulted her center, bit at her clit, wrapped my lips around that sensitive bud and sucked until she cried for me to stop. Here I was now, her hands tangling in my hair as she rides my face, her moans louder and hoarser than I ever would have imagined.

"Don't stop, Machlin. Oh God, please don't stop."

I pin her back harder into the wall as I lift her other leg over my shoulder, bracing her body in the air with my hands on her ass, squeezing as I devour my meal. I quickly thrash back and forth using my tongue, teeth, and lips across her wet pussy and she pulls on my hair, forcing me to look up at her.

She watches my tongue flick against her clit and bites her bottom lip as I bite her back. She pops that plump lip out and clenches her teeth, letting out a low groan as she watches me. I suck her clit into my mouth, popping off with a loud smack. Her eyes are still trained on mine as I take a long lick up her center and then back down with the back of my tongue.

"You like watching me eat this pussy, baby?" I say with a smirk, pressing my lips against her swollen ones.

"Yes," she hisses. "So. Fucking. Hot. Keep going, I'm almost there," she begs, tossing her head back, pushing her body against my mouth harder.

I slip a finger inside her and crook it as my knuckle grazes her ass and she jumps, her eyes opening and looking down at me again.

"Machlin, I--"

"Come for me, Genevieve."

I add another finger and dig my knuckle harder against the opening of her ass as she stares at me, her breathing quick and the loudest moan I've ever elicited from a woman, vibrates off the walls.

"Shit. Damn. Fuckkkkk," she curses through gritted teeth. "Ohhhhhhh."

I wait for her orgasm to ease around my fingers and then carefully place her back on her feet. She wobbles for a second and I catch her as I stand.

Her eyes are hooded, and she reaches for the front of my shorts, rubbing me through the material.

"I guess it's my turn to finally get on my knees, huh?" she smirks.

I put both hands on her shoulders to stop her and move my face closer to hers. Our lips barely touch, and she closes her eyes, expecting a kiss. I try to shut off my brain as it tells me not to give in. If I let her do this, drop to her knees and relieve me, that's only a temporary fix. I leave here and I'll feel lighter but then reality will still come crashing down. I can't escape tonight, even though I really fucking want to. Her orgasm was enough for me, so I pull away from her quickly.

"I'm going to head out."

"You...you're leaving?"

I nod and turn for the front door.

"Goodnight, Genevieve," I say with regret.

I see her jaw flex and she silently nods, backing away from me.

"Goodbye, Machlin."

Chapter 15
Genevieve

I walk into my office, tossing my bag onto my chair and eye the tan shoe box on my desk.

Christian Louboutin. What the hell?

I walk over slowly, opening the box and gasp when I see the classic black, red bottom open toe pumps, shiny as ever.

"You're accompanying me to a benefit tonight," a hard voice states from my doorway.

"Oh, am I? I have my own heels, you know?" I say, slowly turning around.

"I know you do, and I know you can afford these on your own, which was probably your second complaint."

I open my mouth to deny it, but it's true. Dammit.

"Let someone take care of you for a change, Genevieve. Last night wasn't so bad, was it?" Machlin smirks.

"I've had worse," I say, with a sly smile.

He gives me a grin of his own, crossing his arms over his chest.

"Rochelle will be over tonight to watch Kenzie and she's bringing your dress and her hair and makeup woman. I'm coming to get you at seven."

He turns and walks out and I'm stunned into place. Machlin Saddler managed to render me speechless multiple times this week and I don't like it. I don't like it at all.

"Holy. Fuck balls," Rochelle says from behind me.

I glance at myself in the floor length mirror one more time before turning around.

"He knew what the hell he was doing sending me this dress, dammit," I grumble.

The black form fitting gown has lace cutouts on both sides, from the top of my hip to under my arms. More lace attempts to cover my cleavage but fails---hard.

"Well then let your freak flag fly, girl. I don't know what you two are waiting for. This has been seriously going on for *months*. I don't know how you survive with just BOB," Rochelle groans.

"Who the fuck is Bob?"

I snap my head around and my jaw hangs open.

A tuxedo. Of course he fills out a tuxedo like a son-of-a-bitch.

"How the hell did you get into my house?" I ask, with my hands on my hips.

"Rochelle gave me your key in case you ladies were busy with hair and makeup. Don't change the subject, Genevieve. Who the *fuck* is Bob?"

He stomps forward, putting a finger under my chin, forcing my face to look up at him.

"My vibrator, asshole," I snap, slapping his hand off my chin. "We're already starting this night on a great foot. I'm jumping with excitement!" I say, rolling my eyes.

I hear Rochelle giggle as she follows me out of my bedroom and down the stairs.

"Please text me if Kenzie is having a hard time, okay?"

"She'll be fine. I'll lay with her if she has another bad dream. Have fun, Gen, let loose."

She winks and squeezes my shoulder as she walks towards my couch, plopping down.

I exhale, trying to compose myself, and then turn around to a waiting Machlin.

"Ready?"

"Do I have a choice?" I scoff.

He offers me his elbow and I glance at it, raising my eyebrows as I walk past him to my front door. I hear him laugh from behind me and try to ignore the pull I feel in my lower belly. There is no way in hell I am coming out of this night unscathed. Machlin and I both fucking know it.

Machlin

I knew what I was doing sending her that dress, but I didn't fucking care. I *don't* care. Genevieve Langston will be riding my cock by the end of the night. I've tried to be a gentleman--well as close to a gentleman as I can be--but enough is enough. All I think about, day in and day out is Genevieve; her lips, her tits, her ass... everything. I want that calm, that escape, and I'm getting it tonight.

We take the ride in silence, the tension in the air making it impossible to breathe, let alone speak. I pull to the curb and put my car in park as I get out and walk around the other side to open her door. I extend my hand out as she takes it, linking her arm through mine. I toss the key to valet boy as we walk inside, feeling the tension start to ease. Just being next to her, touching her is my salvation.

I greet the people I'm there to see, introduce Genevieve and get my ass kissed for about an hour before my cock is about to burst through my tux zipper. Having Genevieve next to me, smelling her the past hour has driven me insane. I run my hand a little lower on her back, cupping her ass and she turns, pulling on my tie.

"You have an annoying habit of putting your hands where they don't belong, Mr. Saddler," she whispers, through gritted teeth.

"Tell me to piss off, Ms. Langston, I dare you."

She scoffs and rolls her eyes and I reluctantly move my hand higher on her back.

"Let's go somewhere more private," I whisper in her ear.

"I'd rather not," she says back.

I see the defiance in her eyes, and I want to put her in her damn place; on her knees in front of me, sucking my cock.

"And why the fuck not?"

"Because you'll lick my pussy like a timid little cat, instead of devour me like a fucking lion. BOB gives me a better orgasm on the lowest speed," she whispers, then pulls away with a shrug and strides towards the bar.

My jaw is on the floor for a second before I compose myself and grit my teeth. That little...

I finish my whiskey, stomping over to the bar and grab Genevieve's arm, pulling her towards the back of the banquet hall. I open a door, shove her inside and have her pinned against the wall in seconds.

"What the fuck did you just say?" I seethe.

"You. Suck. At. Eating. Pussy," she enunciates.

I smell the whiskey on her breath and smirk.

"You have big balls when you drink, Ms. Langston."

"Bigger than you, Mr. Saddler. When I please a man, I don't do it with a half-assed effort," she challenges, grabbing my crotch and squeezing.

I slam my hand on the wall next to her and press my forehead to hers.

"You're treading in dangerous waters, Genevieve," I warn.

"Let's see who drowns first, shall we?" she responds, arching an eyebrow.

In one movement I lift her, spinning her around and dropping her on top of a desk. My hands land on her breasts and my lips touch her earlobe, biting it. I hear her suck in a breath when I roughly part her legs to stand in between them.

"I'm done with the teasing, Genevieve. Right here with a room full of benefactors within earshot, I am finally taking you. Let them all know who they're here for. I want to hear you scream my name, loud and proud."

"How about you make me," she grinds out, grabbing my jaw.

I slam my hand down on her thigh, making her jump and a squeal escapes her lips.

"Oh, Ms. Langston, I have waited for this moment for months. You will leave this room thoroughly fucked and I don't care how long it fucking takes. I have nowhere else to be except in between these thighs."

I don't wait for a response; for her to tell me to fuck myself or to tell me no. I slam my lips into hers, fumbling underneath her dress with her thong and shredding it, tossing it to the floor. She lets out a small yell and I'm there again, devouring her mouth as I move her hand to unzip my pants.

"Take me out and stroke me. Put your money where your mouth is, Langston."

She jumps to her feet, pushing off me as she turns us, slamming my ass to the desk.

"You need a lesson, Mr. Saddler..." Her gaze never wavers from mine as she unbuckles my belt and unzips my pants, slowly...so fucking slowly.

I watch as she pulls down my briefs, my thick, angry cock springing free and her eyes still stay locked on mine.

"I was right about one thing," she says sexily, stroking my erection.

I lean my head back and moan at the pleasure coursing through my veins at her first touch.

"What's that?" I groan.

"Your big-dick personality matches the equipment," she admits, squeezing the base of my cock.

I let out a rough laugh but then it's caught in my throat as I feel her warm mouth envelop me. Within seconds, I'm at the back of her throat and I swallow a low growl, threatening to break free.

"Holy fuck, Genevieve."

Her tongue wraps around my shaft as she moves her mouth up and down, her hand squeezing my base, matching her movements. She hollows out her cheeks, sucking the fucking life out of me and I grit my teeth, my fingers itching to grab her head and fuck her mouth. It's torture, her skilled tongue and lips working my shaft to its breaking point and I look down, realizing she's been watching me. Our eyes lock as her mouth is full of my cock, and I drop my chin, taking in the euphoria. I feel her sharp nail run along my jaw and lift my face as she pops off.

"Watch me," she whispers.

Hell if I don't just come right then and there. She drags her tongue up the side of my shaft like a lollipop and then around my crown, moving to the other side and doing it again. I growl as she grabs my balls in her hand, sucking one in her mouth, then the other. She devours my cock again and I'm done for, trying to grab her hair, to pull her up so I don't blow my load down her damn throat. She smacks my hand away instead, popping off my dick with a loud pop.

"At least one of us knows how to eat," she smirks, getting to her feet.

She reaches for the back of my neck, but I grab her wrist and spin her, pushing her down on the desk. Her chest slams hard against the wood and her ass is lined up perfectly in front of my face. I pull her dress up, spanking her bare ass and she squeals.

"I had you writhing on my face in your house, don't fucking deny it, Genny, but because I'm a giving man, I'll remind you how good it was."

I grab onto both of her ass cheeks, squeezing them hard in my hands as I kneel down and suck her pussy lips into my mouth. She bucks up against the desk, gripping the edge and I grasp her ass harder, pulling her body down onto my mouth. I slam my tongue inside her, coating her walls as I move one hand to her front, pressing my thumb to her clit.

"Oh God, Machlin, like that," she whines.

I growl, thrashing my face back and forth against her soaking center, and then slip two fingers inside her channel. I roughly push them in and out, faster and faster as I feel Genevieve shake above me.

"Too...much, Mac...I...oh holy fuck, I..."

I add a third, pushing them in and out of her at an inhuman pace as my tongue works on the tight rim of her ass. She jumps, slamming her hand on the desk with a scream.

"Machlin!"

Her walls squeeze my fingers, immobilizing them as she rides out her orgasm and drops her head to the desk with a loud thunk! I don't give her time to recover as I stand, replacing my fingers with my cock and pistoning into her. She makes me fucking crazy and I want to punish her with all the pleasure I can possibly give. Too much, I don't want her to be able to handle it. I want her to beg me to stop. The pain in my ass that I need to fuck out of my system. I want to punish her for making me feel things I can't feel, I *shouldn't* feel.

"Machlin, wait...wait, I...oh my God..."

"You wanted the lion, Genny. You got the fucking lion. Fuck, you feel so good."

I slap her ass then grab onto her cheeks again as I thrust into her, moving the desk into the wall, aware that all the benefit guests can probably hear our fucking, but I don't care. The echo of skin slapping against skin fills the room and I brace both hands on her lower back, pulling her body back and forth against mine, using her like a doll.

"Turn me around," she pants.

I can't do that. I can't see her face while I fuck her, but she doesn't care. She pushes her body back, taking me off guard as I slip out of her. She turns around quickly, laying her back on the desk, looking up at me expectantly.

"Are you going to finish fucking me or just stare at me?" she asks with a grin.

That's it. The moment that I knew Genevieve was going to be the woman I never forgot. I brace my hands above her shoulders on the desk and push into her slowly, her legs wrapping around my waist and she lets out a slow, satisfied groan.

"Yessss," she hisses. "Like this."

My body rubs against her clit and I already feel her body squeezing me as I watch her face surrender to the bliss.

Her mouth circles and there's a crease in between her eyebrows and suddenly I'm doing more than fucking her. I'm *studying* her, I'm committing all of this to memory because I know it can't happen again, it *shouldn't* happen again.

Her orgasm smacks me out of my thoughts as she squeezes me tight and I can't control my own. I drop down to her chest, groaning loudly as I empty myself inside her, grinding until I feel the numbness subside.

I try and catch my breath before I lean up, getting to my feet and start to put myself back together. I hear Genevieve start to giggle and I turn around, my eyebrows furrowed.

"What the hell are you laughing at?"

She smoothes her dress then pulls her hair out in front of it, sauntering over to me.

"All this time I thought *you* were the big, bad wolf." She winks and starts to walk away from me, but I take quick steps and catch up to her.

"What the fuck does that even mean?"

"You're so easy, Machlin Saddler. So. Damn. Easy," she says poking my chest with each word. "Your pride is so enormous that it blocks your ability to detect my bullshit. It's okay big guy, we can't all be gorgeous and smart." She pats my chest and gives me another wink.

She turns and walks away, and I cannot believe what the fuck just happened. She played me like a goddamn fiddle. I came here tonight knowing I would finally have her, but she riled me up to make sure. I guess I'm not done with Genevieve Langston because fuck if I let her have the last word.

Genevieve

I reach for the radio dial in Machlin's car, but he slaps my hand down.

"That was rude!" I protest.

"Don't touch a man's radio, Genny."

"I cannot listen to this! I'm getting a headache!"

"If you can't listen to Black Sabbath, then this relationship will never work," he smirks.

"We have no relationship, Machlin." I roll my eyes.

"I'm pretty sure the guests at the benefit would have something different to say. Don't act like you didn't work BOB up a frenzy this morning after dreaming about me all night."

I laugh and cross my arms over my chest, pretending I did no such thing.

"Whatever," I mutter.

"Ha! Knew it. Down for a repeat whenever you are, baby," he whispers, as he pulls into the driveway.

I don't answer as he cuts the engine and I get out of the truck, walking towards the trunk. I open the latch, but Machlin's hand is there, stopping me.

"Is that a yes or a no?" he whispers from behind me, his lips against my ear.

He moves my ponytail off my neck with his nose and then buries his face against my skin. I moan at the friction from his facial hair, my sensitive neck waiting for him to pounce...hoping he will.

He turns me around quickly, lifting me to sit in the bed of the truck and stands between my legs, lifting my thigh to wrap around his waist. I squeal and lean my hands back, catching myself from falling on my back.

"Yes. Or. No," he repeats.

Stay strong, Genevieve. Stay strong. Last night was last night, don't let him rile you up!

"No. That's a no," I say with zero conviction.

He smiles, knowing I'll fall and instead of being a gentleman--which he certainly is not--he pushes.

"No?"

His strong hand slides up my thigh and I close my eyes at the contact. He squeezes as he gets higher and higher and when he slips his fingers inside the hem of my shorts, I let him.

I let him slide my thong to the side and thrust his finger into my wet center. I let him press his lips to mine, as he pushes another finger inside of me and slowly makes me fall.

"Yesssss," I sigh, dropping my forehead to his shoulder.

I'm about to explode on his fingers--surrender to him again--when my cell phone rings from my hip holster. I frantically push him away, his fingers slipping out of me as I answer the call from an unknown number.

"Genevieve Langston," I say out of breath.

"Hi Genevieve, this is Patty, your mother's next-door neighbor."

My stomach drops and I push Machlin back as I get to my feet, pacing next to the truck.

"H-Hi. What's going on, is she okay?"

"She's okay, she just...is causing somewhat of a scene and we really don't want to call the cops. Maybe it's best if you come on over here."

I close my eyes and let out a sigh of relief that she's okay, but then the stress creeps up when I register her words. Shit.

"Of course, thank you for calling me first. I'm on my way over," I say, as I walk towards the passenger door and motion for Machlin to follow.

"What happened?" he asks as we both get into the truck.

"I...just have to go to my mom's quick. You can drop me at the office, and I'll grab my car, then I can come back after and help you--"

"We'll go straight there," he interrupts. "Is she okay?"

"I'd rather we didn't," I groan. "My mom is...struggling. I'd rather just go alone."

"Genn, it's going to take an hour for us to do all this dropping off and going back and forth. I'll wait in the car and I won't get in the way."

His mind is made up and when Machlin Saddler wants something, he gets it. There's no point in even arguing.

"Fine. But just...wait in the car."

I give him directions as we take the ten-minute drive and groan as I see my mom on the front porch wielding a bottle of whiskey like a baseball bat, two neighbors out on her front lawn.

"Don't move," I warn Machlin, pointing my finger at him.

He puts his hands in the air as I get out of the car and walk towards my mother.

"Mama, let's go inside. What are you doing?"

I walk over to her as she points the empty bottle at the two women on the front lawn.

"Those homewreckers want a piece of me! I'll show you bitches!"

I guide her into the house as she walks backwards, still pointing the bottle at the ladies. I shut the door behind us and take the empty bottle from her hand.

"Mama, what are you doing? They were going to call the cops on you!"

"Ironic," she whispers.

I close my eyes and shake my head as I guide her to her bedroom.

"Do you want me to put the TV on for you? I'll come back later with dinner, okay? I'm just finishing up work for a few more hours."

She doesn't respond. She lays in bed and rolls over, giving me her back. I sigh and walk out, shutting the door behind me. I lean against it, letting out a breath as I collect myself. Everyday it's something, I just need a break.

I walk down the hall and of course see Machlin, standing in front of the fireplace, looking at the pictures on the mantle.

"You don't know how to do what you're told, do you?" I snap.

"And you do? I didn't know your father was a police officer." he says, turning around.

"Well then your Saddler Enterprises background check team needs to be replaced. His death was all over the local paper. He was a Detective, actually."

"Is that how he--"

"I don't want to talk about this. We have shit to do, let's go," I say, walking to the front door.

I don't wait for him to follow as I turn the lock on the knob and walk towards the truck, hopping up inside and trying to push down the hurt. I can't, it doesn't work.

I watch as Machlin shuts the front door and walks towards the truck and I feel it...the need to escape. I hate that he's the one to give it to me but right now, I don't care how I get it. I just need it.

He gets inside and as he starts the truck, I reach over, grabbing his crotch through his jeans.

"Pull over somewhere. We have unfinished business."

He looks over at me, arching an eyebrow and I see the pity in his gaze. I don't want that fucking look, I want the desire.

"Or you can drive, and I can take care of it myself," I say, leaning back in my seat and unbuttoning my shorts.

His hand slamming against mine stops me and I look up at him again and this time I see what I want.

Desire. It's raw, fierce, desire. That's the look I want, the look that will push me to escape.

He moves his hand to the back of my head and pulls on my ponytail, bringing my face to his. As he pulls to the side of the empty road and unbuckles his seatbelt, he presses his lips to my ear.

"Don't you fucking dare."

Chapter 16
Machlin

"Come to the fair with me tonight...you and Kenzie," I say, from the doorway of Genevieve's office.

"What? Why in the hell would I do that?" she says incredulously.

"Because I want zeppoles and I don't want to look like a fucking child molester going by myself. I'll have a car pick you both up at fo--"

"No!"

My eyebrows are up to my hairline as I watch her smile lift.

"No?"

"If we're going to the fair, then we'll go like normal people. *You* can pick up me and Kenzie in *your* car. We'll be ready," she says, with a cheesy smile.

I return one and shake my head.

"Fine, brat! P.S I got you something."

I smirk, closing her office door behind me and walk over to her with the coffee mug I bought the other day.

I make my way to her side of the desk, pushing her chair back and roughly push her legs open.

"Machlin! What in the hell are you--"

"Say thank you for the mug, Genevieve."

I get to my knees in front of her as I watch her eyebrows pull together.

"I sleep with the boss! Really? Where the hell did you even get this?" she snaps, lifting the mug in the air.

"At the store. It was fate. Now shut the hell up so I can make you come. I didn't lock the door..."

"Mac, you can't--"

I shut her up with a rip right through her thong and then drop my head, hungrily diving into her center, lifting her leg over my shoulder.

"Oh f-fuck, Machlin!"

Her hands grip my hair, messing the perfectly gelled style and I watch as she grits her teeth, digging her heel into my back.

I suck on one of her pussy lips, nibbling the skin and she gasps, looking down at me.

"What the...hell did you just...do," she pants.

I smile, doing it to the other lip and then latch onto her clit, sucking it into my mouth and nibbling on that too. Her gasps, her heavy breathing, her soft moans make me hard as a fucking brick in my pants.

"Oh God, oh God, oh God," she chants. "I'm so close, Machlin. Fuck, I'm so close."

I hear her door suddenly open and then her legs are clamped around my neck as she gasps, leaning forward.

"R-rochelle, don't you knock?" Genevieve says out of breath.

"I never knock. What are you doing for lunch?" Rochelle asks, her heels clacking on the floor.

Genevieve leans forward more, her elbows on her desk, pushing her pussy further into my face. I smile against her as she pulls on my hair to keep me away.

Not happening.

"I um...I don't know. I'll text you when I'm done working," she says, as I lick up her thigh.

She flinches, banging her knee on the desk and I grab her thighs with both hands, spreading her for me again.

"What the hell is wrong with you?" Rochelle asks.

"N-nothing, I'm just tired, I..."

"Oh my God. Where did you get that mug!" Rochelle gasps. "You're fucking my brother?" she yells excitedly.

"Oh my God, Rochelle, shut up!"

I lunge for her lips, slipping my tongue inside her center and then add a finger, not giving her any reprieve. I hear her stifle a whimper and then another gasp.

"Oh hell no. Is...Machlin, are you under Genn's desk?" Rochelle laughs.

"Rochelle! Just...shut the door on your way out. I'll text you for lunch...like...five minutes," she struggles to say.

"I called this!" Rochelle says, in a sing song voice as I hear the door shut.

"I'm going to kill you," Genevieve whisper yells through gritted teeth, lifting my face.

I grab her wrists and pin them down to the arm rests as I finally finish her, thrashing against her as she struggles to catch her breath. My tongue, teeth and lips, assaulting her until she's riding my face, lifting her body up to my mouth and warm, sweet, juice drips from her pussy lips.

"Mmmm, my God. That felt so good."

I stand, giving her a wink and walk towards the door.

"Wait! I...I wanna suck your cock, Machlin. Get back here."

I turn and see her standing with her hands on her hips and laugh.

"I have a conference call. Rain check, gorgeous."

I walk out towards my office and realize I'm smiling like a fucking idiot. Ever since the benefit a few nights ago, Genevieve and I have spent every waking minute together. Every time we part it feels like a part of myself is going with her and I fucking hate it. I could have easily texted her to ask about tonight, but I needed to see her again, feel her again. It's like my body needs the reprieve I get from her.

I should keep it just sex between us, but I know she can't leave Kenzie again tonight.

The fair was something my siblings and I have enjoyed every year since we were kids and when I saw the flyer on my way into work today, Kenzie was all I thought about.

Genn told me she was having nightmares again the past few nights, which was how Genn ended up on my desk with her legs spread yesterday morning; using me to escape her stresses, just as much as I'm using her. I wanted to give her that escape again today, feeling the change in her after we part. Her smile is brighter, her eyes clearer, her face relaxed. It's not healthy what we're doing, we should stop, but I know I can't and I'm sure it's the same for her.

Bringing Kenzie to this fair will maybe help her out of her negative thoughts. The family therapist we saw for a while always told us to remember the happy times, do things to keep busy, keep yourself happy. What kid isn't happy at a fair? The fact that I'm trying to make Kenzie happy should be a warning sign, but I ignore it. I'm just being a good guy, making sure my employee starts to get better sleep, so she is at the top of her game. At least that's the lie I tell myself.

"Look at this beautiful lady. Hey cutie," I say, lifting Kenzie as she runs into my arms.

"Hi, Man!"

"You ready to have some fun?" I ask.

She nods enthusiastically as I put her down on her feet, taking her car seat from Genevieve's hands.

"You clean up good too, Langston," I smirk.

"Shut it, Saddler," she says, rolling her eyes.

She lifts Kenzie as I buckle in her car seat and then put her in, strapping her up. I open Genevieve's door for her, and she shakes her head with a laugh.

"Trying to go for a doubleheader today, buddy?" she asks, arching an eyebrow.

"You know I'm never too fatigued for you, *Genny,*" I whisper.

She slaps at my chest as she leans down and sits in the passenger seat and I shut the door, walking around to the other side.

We drive to the fair in silence, the radio the only sound filling the car. This is weird. Really, really weird but at the same time it feels...good. I pull my car into a spot on the grass and cut the engine as Genevieve and I get out. She takes Kenzie out of the car seat and immediately, she runs towards me.

"Up, Man!" She lifts her arms for me to hold her.

I laugh and lift her easily, putting her on my shoulders.

"Too high or good?" I ask.

"Good!" she says, patting the top of my head.

I glance down at Genevieve and she has a smile I haven't seen on her before. It isn't her sassy, shit eating grin or her practiced smile she gives to clients, it's real... a real smile and it sucker punches me. I thought the sparring Genevieve was my downfall, but this one...this one is my undoing.

"Mac?"

"Yeah...what?" I ask, breaking myself out of my thoughts.

"I said are we getting you your zeppoles first, or do you want to do rides and games?"

"We can do rides and games first. Ladies first, always," I say with a sly smile.

"Hmmmm, that wasn't your MO yesterday morning," she mumbles.

I lower my head to whisper in her ear.

"If you listened to me when I told you to stop squeezing my cock, I wouldn't have blown my load so fast."

She lets out a low sigh and mumbles what sounds like "asshole" under her breath.

"What was that, Ms. Langston? Did you say something?" I ask, stopping in front of her.

Kenzie laughs from above me and Genn pushes at my shoulder.

"I said, rides sound great, *Mr. Saddler*," she responds with her cheesy, fake smile.

I laugh and shake my head as we walk towards the fair, buying tickets for the rides.

"What's first, cutie?" I ask, dropping Kenzie to her feet.

She points at a train ride and we walk over as she reaches for both mine and Genevieve's hands.

"I don't think I'm going to be able to go on this one," I laugh, looking at the tiny train cars that not even my right leg would fit in.

"I'm not sure if I'm even allowed on," Genevieve says, looking at the sign by the ride entrance. "Actually. Yep. I can. Let's go, big girl," Genn says, pulling Kenzie to the front of the line.

I hand them both tickets over the railing and the attendant takes them, opening the gate for them to enter. I watch as Genevieve lets Kenzie pick out the train car and lift her inside, strapping them both in. The ride starts and Kenzie squeals, waving to me.

"Hi Man!" she yells, a big smile on her face.

I laugh, loving that she always calls me man and wave back to her.

"Looking good ladies," I yell back.

Genevieve laughs, putting her arm around Kenzie as I watch them take the track a few more times. Each second I watch them, it pulls me further and further into happiness. This should be an easy solution. Kenzie and Genn make me happy. I should start something, see where it goes--simple-- but of course it never is.

The ride stops and Genn lifts Kenzie, walking back over to me.

"What next?" Genn asks.

Kenzie points to the Ferris Wheel and I nod as we walk over, holding Kenzie's hand in between us.

"So how many years apart are all you Saddler's?" Genevieve asks.

"I'm thirty-two, Elijah and Val are thirty, Rochelle is twenty-six and Dakota is twenty."

"You guys watched Disney movies that old, huh?" she asks.

"It was...a girl thing they did with my mom when they were younger. Every Saturday night was Disney night. They stopped when they were older and made it into movie night instead, but when my mom passed...they felt like it was their way to be with her, I guess."

I can see her eyes sadden and she shakes her head.

"I'm sorry, Mac. I didn't mean for that to come out the way it did."

I pinch her cheek with my other hand and furrow my brows.

"You didn't know, Genny. I know you didn't mean it in a malicious way."

I can see the wheels in her head turning still and she feels bad. This is weird for us, being civil without the sarcasm and back talk. It's different but...nice.

"Kenzie's really happy, you know. You're doing a great job with her," I say, breaking her out of her guilt.

Genevieve looks up and opens her mouth but then shuts it, giving me a sad smile.

"Thank you for saying that. It means a lot. Some days I...don't know, but...thank you."

I nod at her sincerity, her vulnerability and every damn thing about this woman intrigues me. Her soft side, her bitch side, her badass side... everything. I'm torturing myself today, but I have to remember the smile on Kenzie's face. This is for her, not me. It's never about me.

"Thank you for tonight, we had a great time," Genn says as I take her keys and unlock her door.

Kenzie is asleep in her arms as we walk inside and she nods to upstairs.

"I'll get going, lock up behind me."

"You're going?" she asks with confusion.

I nod as I walk towards the front door and shut it behind me, not saying another word. Tonight was a lot and if I stayed--if I used Genevieve, buried myself inside her--it wouldn't be just physical. I have to try to start dealing with all of this on my own.

Chapter 17
Machlin

I'm sitting at my desk, head down on top of it, trying to get sleep. I'm exhausted. Carrying around all this weight is beating me down, slowly...day by day.

"Son, you need to wake up. Everyone needs you to wake up!"

I snap my head up and see my father standing in the doorway of my office.

"Dad?" My eyebrows pull together with confusion because that's definitely my father. "What are you doing here?"

"Reminding you how important you are to this family, to the company. You're getting distracted, son. Everyone needs you, everyone needs you to remember what's important."

I stand, walking over to him as I nod.

"I know what's important. I promise I won't let you down. I have everything under control, I can handle all this," I say, with a determined tone.

He shakes his head with a smile, putting his hand on my shoulder.

"Then handle it, son. Val is hurting, Elijah needs guidance, Rochelle is hurting too on the inside and Dakota, too, is in so much need. So many people need you, Machlin...so many..."

I watch as he slowly starts to disappear, and I try and reach for him, but he's gone.

"Dad! Dad..."

I startle awake in bed and feel the tears start to form in my eyes. I drop my head into my hands, knowing I can't allow myself to feel the grief, I don't have time for this. I glance at my phone on the nightstand.

12:01.

I don't give myself time to think as I dial Genevieve's number and wait as it rings, ignoring the pull to just hang up and go back to bed.

"Mac?" she answers in a sleepy voice. "What's wrong?"

"Unlock your door, I'm coming over. I'll be there in five minutes."

I hang up, not letting her answer as I quickly throw on shorts and a t-shirt. I brush my teeth quickly, jogging downstairs and out to my car as I drive the few minutes to her house. I pull into Genevieve's driveway and notice Kenzie's car seat still in the back of my car from the fair a few hours ago. I get out, unbuckle her seat and walk to the front door as Genevieve opens the door.

"Really, Mac? I could have gotten the car seat tomorrow, it's freaking past midn--"

I cut off her rant with my lips as I push into the house, dropping the car seat to the floor and shutting the door behind me. I lift Genevieve in my arms and start to walk us to the couch, but she breaks the kiss, stopping me.

"My bed," she pants. "I finally want you in a damn bed."

Shit. That's exactly what I didn't want, but the itch to disappear for a little while creeps up my spine. Just do it, Machlin.

I nod as I latch onto her neck, licking against her pulse, her heartbeat rapid against my chest. She reaches for the hem of my t-shirt and pulls it over my head as I walk up the stairs. She drops it on the top step and then leans back, whipping off her own as I grip her ass, holding her up.

She drops her shirt to the hallway floor as I walk into her bedroom and shut the door behind me, locking it.

I slam her back to the bed as I fall on top of her, bracing my weight on my hands above her head.

"Take me out of these shorts and fuck me from underneath. I want to watch you wriggle and thrust this little body so fucking fast against my cock."

She closes her eyes, nodding silently as she moves her skimpy pajama shorts to the side, then frees me from my own.

I'm so hard that my cock bounces off my stomach as she pulls my shorts down, grabbing behind for my balls. She massages them in her hands, watching my face as I slowly succumb to her.

"Inside you," I groan. "Put me inside you, Genny."

She moves the head of my cock to her entrance and I keep my eyes open with everything I have, just to watch her face as she takes me...as I fill her.

"God, you feel so good. I love fucking you, dammit. Fuckkkkk," I groan.

I look down at where our bodies are connected and watch Genevieve start to move her hips up and down as she grips

181

my back with her long nails. She's taking from me, grinding against me faster, and faster as I brace myself above her, letting her. Her legs wrap tighter around my back as she thrusts her body up against me and back down, her walls starting to constrict.

I look down again and see half my dick not even inside her and I push down against her movements, eliciting a gasp.

"Take all of me," I growl.

"I...c-cant, Mac," she gasps, as I push a little more into her.

"Fuck that, yes you can."

I roll us over quickly and Genevieve's hands slap to my chest to stop herself from falling. She's still not seated all the way down on me and I push up fast and hard as she drops her head to my chest, panting.

"It's too...much," she whispers.

I grab her face, pulling it up to look at me and her gaze is hooded. Those long eyelashes covering those chocolate eyes and I smile, shaking my head.

"You handle this big dick on a daily basis like a champ, Genny," I say, pointing at myself. "Now handle this one," I say as I thrust up into her.

"Ohhh Goddd," she moans, dropping her head back.

I lean up on my hands, moving myself to a sitting position as Genevieve starts to grind on my lap, taking in another inch of me with every movement.

I wrap my arm around her waist as the other fists her hair and pulls it back, exposing her neck so I can feast on it.

Her hands fall to my shoulders as she moves on top of me, moaning each time I pull on her hair. I place soft kisses on her neck, then I'm biting her, sucking her until she starts mumbling incoherent words.

"Close...the best...I...can't...yes...there."

She starts to squeeze me, and I drop her to the bed, slamming her back down on the mattress as I unleash on her, pistoning myself into her as she cries out and loses herself. Fuck if I lose my damn mind too as I watch her face, that beautiful look she has when I make her come. I feel the tranquility take me as I pull myself out, fisting my cock and shoot my load all over her bare breasts.

My groan is loud as I watch the liquid pool in between them and instantly, I want to take her again.

"You're the worst, Machlin Saddler," she complains in a sleepy voice.

I hop off the bed quick, opening the bedroom door as I grab my shirt off the hallway floor and come back to clean her up.

"Marking you as mine, Langston...until I say otherwise," I say with a smile, leaning over her and pushing her hair off her forehead.

"Stay," she whispers.

I watch as her eyes close, and her breathing evens out and realize she's probably exhausted. I'm so fucking selfish, using her to help me when she's got plenty of her own shit going on.

I glance around her room and spot a notebook with a pen on a desk. I open it to the back, ripping off a piece of paper and write out a note for her.

Pain in my ass,
Take the day off tomorrow and sleep in with Kenzie. Spend
time with her and be lazy. Food will be delivered for
breakfast, lunch and dinner so don't you dare cook. I
expect you freshly relaxed and ready to work in two days.
See you then,
Mac

I put it on her nightstand and reach for her phone, sliding
to unlock the screen. I shut off all her alarms and then take
one last look at her.

She looks so...young when she's sleeping. No worries, no
sadness, just *peace*. I shake my head as I walk downstairs
without a shirt, my hair a mess and cock still hard beneath
my shorts. The controlled Machlin Saddler would smack
this one in the face for not being able to compartmentalize
his shit.

Walking back to my car, I lock her front door on my way
out. I'm on a runaway roller coaster with Genevieve
Langston and I don't know how the fuck I'm getting off.

Chapter 18
Machlin

"I'm going to look through all accounts Jeremy has worked on again and sift through them to look for the bank representative. If it was Whitney Roark then pull it, that's all we have right now," I say, throwing my pen on my desk.

"Can I ask why you stopped this undercover shit if you didn't really have everything you needed with Jeremy?" Rochelle asks.

I glance over at Genevieve and then back at Rochelle as Elijah snorts. I can't admit out loud that I pulled the plug too early because I couldn't lie to Genevieve anymore. It would solidify that I care about her more than I should and give her false hope that we could ever be something serious. We can't.

"We do...almost. He was getting suspicious," I lie. "Genevieve, you'll stay and put in overtime with me," I say, glancing over to the other side of my desk, changing the subject.

Her gaze snaps up, her pen freezes on her notebook as she arches an eyebrow at me.

"Overtime, huh?"

"Rochelle, could you get Kenzie from the childcare center and bring her back home with you? Genevieve and I will swing by your place on the ride home. We won't be too late."

"Sure thing, *boss*," Rochelle answers, with a knowing grin.

She gets to her feet, as does Elijah.

"Genn, if he tries anything, I give you full permission to kick him in the balls," Elijah warns, pointing a finger at me.

Genevieve laughs.

"I can handle him," she says, with a mischievous grin.

Elijah and Rochelle leave the room and the second the door is closed, I lunge for her, jumping over my desk as she reaches for my tie, loosening it.

I reach underneath her skirt and rip her thong off her and put it in my pocket as she moans, sucking my bottom lip between her teeth. I push her down, slamming her back onto my desk, pulling a gasp from her red painted lips.

"God, I've missed this pussy," I groan.

"And I've missed your cock."

It's only been a day, but a day is too long. The case is at a standstill and I need my drug, my distraction away from this shit, as does she.

The phone ringing on my desk makes Genevieve jump and I nod towards it.

"Answer the phone, Genevieve."

"But...we were...y-you have my panties in your--"

"Answer. The. Phone."

She lets out a frustrated sigh and then points at me.

"Be good!"

I give her a devilish smile and I start to unbutton my shirt, watching her eyelids flutter closed.

"Saddler Enterprises, Machlin Saddler's office," she says in a breathy tone, as she watches me take off my shirt and slowly unzip my pants.

She nods to the person on the phone and I run a finger up the inside of her thigh. I watch her dig her teeth into her bottom lip, trying to contain her reaction.

"Words, Genny. They can't see you."

"I...yes of c-course we'll set up a meeting," she stutters.

Her eyes close as I get to the apex of her thighs, parting them as I inch up her skirt.

"Y-yes we have t-time tomorrow. What were you...thinking?" she struggles to say.

"I didn't sleep but a minute last night," I groan, kissing up her thigh. "I need to be inside you again. I always need to be inside you, dammit."

She whimpers and I look up, slapping the inside of her thigh as she flinches.

"Those sounds are for me and me only. Control. It," I snap.

"I can't, you asshole," she whispers through gritted teeth, putting her hand over the receiver.

"A l-lunch meeting sounds great," she responds with a hoarse voice, as she grips my hair.

I run my finger through her wet folds, and she throws her head back, her mouth opening.

"If you want that to be my tongue, fucking control it."

She silently nods, her eyes fire as she watches me take out my cock and stroke it. I see her lick her lips and smile.

"Y-yes Bistro 9 is f-fine, we'll see you there at o-one."

She slams the phone down and grabs my chin, bringing my face up to hers.

"Fuck me," she whispers, pulling on my hair as she devours my mouth. "Right now."

I nod, lining my dick up with her entrance and push into her hard, as I move the desk with my thrust. My hands engulf her tiny waist as I move her up and down on my shaft, watching the place where our bodies connect. I open her lips, finding her sensitive bud and press on it, starting to move my thumb as fast as my body.

"Oh God, too much, Machlin!"

"Come, Genny. I'm going to fuck you against that wall so come, right now," I grit out.

She grabs my hand that's flicking her clit and moves hers down next to mine, both of us bringing her to the edge. Watching her take control, watching her fingers move even faster than my own is so fucking hot. I steal a glance at her face and it's in my favorite expression.

Pure. Fucking. Ecstasy.

"Oh yesssss, yessss, right there."

Our fingers move faster as I piston into her, my hands gripping her soft skin. She tightens around me with a low, drawn out moan and I pull her up in my arms. I walk us to the wall as I unleash everything into her, pumping my body hard into hers and she drops her arms over my shoulders, her forehead dropping to mine.

"Harder," she whispers. "Fuck me as hard as you can, Machlin Saddler."

Her voice is drained but I do what she asks, planting my feet on the floor and wreck her, our bodies slapping against each other and I feel myself falling. Jeremy is long gone, my responsibilities are nonexistent, it's just her and me and the relief crashes into me.

My legs tense and I let out a loud breath, my pace frantic as I unload inside her body, our breathing ragged and rough.

She drops her head to my shoulder, and I carry her to my desk, sitting on my chair with her on my lap. My cock twitches inside her but she doesn't move.

"Genny?" I grab her cheeks to lift her face and her eyes slowly open. "Are you okay?"

"That was crazy," she smiles, shaking her head. "Truthfully, I think I passed out before you finished."

"Jesus. You told me to go harder!"

"It was good, Mac. Maybe even made me retract my, 'you suck at eating pussy' statement."

I laugh and shake my head, cupping her cheeks.

"You need to eat during your lunch break, I know you don't," I reprimand.

"I had the Grossman account and then the Ha--"

"I don't give a fuck. That can be dealt with after lunch. Don't skip a meal again, do you understand?"

She rolls her eyes and slaps my hands off her cheeks. Back to the sass; my favorite flavor.

"Yes, yes. Got it. Now get out of me," she says, slapping at my chest.

I laugh as I lift her off my lap, slipping out of her and she gasps.

"Fuck, Machlin, we keep forgetting a condom."

She grabs tissues from the side of my desk and cleans herself up before throwing them in the trash.

"I'm clean, if that's what you're worried about," I say, zipping myself back up in my pants.

"How about a damn baby? You weren't worried about that?"

"You're not on the pill?"

"Not all women are on the pill, jackass. Don't make assumptions!"

"I...well okay we...shit..." I feel my face go white and fast forward to a baby with Genevieve.

It fucking terrifies me and I want to throw up until I hear her laughing.

"Why are you fucking laughing again? I amuse you, huh?" I growl.

"Your face! Oh my God!" she says, pointing at me and continuing to laugh. "I'm on the pill. Relax, but don't assume next time!" she says, her expression serious now as she slaps my chest.

"I'll order takeout for us," I grumble, picking up my phone and dialing for food.

I watch as Genevieve sits at the chair opposite my desk and starts filing through a folder at the same time she swipes through the I-Pad.

"Food should be here soon. Do you always work yourself to death or is that because you're trying to spend as little time with me as possible?" I ask, crossing my arms over my chest.

She looks up with her eyebrows furrowed.

"I do want to get home to Kenzie, but I also just work like this all the time. I have two hands and two eyes, might as well use them both."

I sit and watch her as she continues, scanning the folder one second then swiping the next.

"So that vacation time you complained about...that true?" I ask, remembering her conversation with Adam.

"Everything I told you was true, Machlin," she says without looking up.

"Everything I said to you was true, also. I may have been wearing a mustache, wig and contacts but everything else was me."

She looks up, observing me for a fault, but she won't get one. I was telling the truth. Every last detail.

"What's the name of the song Sleeping Beauty sings in the forest when she meets Prince Phillip?"

I smile and shake my head.

"Tell anyone I know this information and you'll pay," I warn, arching my eyebrow.

She smiles, putting her hands up in defense.

"Once Upon a Dream."

She opens her mouth but then closes it, silently nodding then turning back to her work.

"That's it? That's the test? What about everything else I told you?" I laugh.

"I did my senior thesis on you and Saddler Enterprises, Machlin. I know you weren't lying about the rest. My detective skills are lacking though. I don't know how I didn't figure it out sooner. Thinking back now, there were so many times it was obvious, especially the tattoo remark."

"I thought you would too, honestly. I mean I changed my voice but...I thought you would at least remember the feel of my lips," I whisper, walking closer to her.

She looks up through her lashes, watching me make my way towards her.

"It was the mustache...I never did get to ride it," she smirks.

"And you're never going to. Fuck that," I growl.

"Machlin Saddler...are you jealous of *yourself*?" she smirks.

Before I can answer, my cell phone rings and I try to ignore it as I cup Genevieve's cheek and kiss her. I don't know what the hell we're doing here, but I can't stop. It's like she's my drug and it's cliched as fuck but she is. She's my escape and no matter how many times I try to tell myself to stop, I can't. It's the only way I can escape the burdens without hurting anyone...anyone except maybe Genevieve.

My cell phone rings again, and I groan, breaking the kiss and reaching into my pocket to fish it out.

Valentina.

"Val, hey! What's going on?"

"Hi, Mac," my sister says.

Her voice is tired...sad and I know she loves traveling, but I know she misses home. Too bad *home* reminds her of my asshole ex-best friend that broke her heart.

"What's going on, sis?"

"I...I'm gonna be home for a little bit. How's everyone doing?"

"We're all the same, how are you?" I ask, sitting on the edge of my desk.

"I'm...good. Really good. I'm in Portugal right now, then I don't have anything planned for the next few months."

"Few months, huh? You'd stay here for a few months?" I ask curiously.

Val has never stayed for more than a week at a time and the time spent home is with us or at the pub. This town destroys her, and it kills me every single time she comes home. The desire to stay with her family, but the heartbreak she goes through.

"I mean I have my house so...might as well right?"

It would be a miracle if she lasted even a week. I hear the strain in her voice...the panic and I sigh.

"Val, why don't you--"

"Don't, Machlin. Don't lecture me. If that's how it's going to be, I'll find another gig. There's plenty out there, I just thought it would be nice to see everyone."

"Okay, okay, no lecture. Let me know when you book a flight and I'll send a car to pick you up. I love you, be careful."

"Love you, too. See you soon."

I sigh, shutting my phone and run my hand down my face. I momentarily forgot the load I carry on my shoulders. All the people in my family I need to take care of, keep happy and make sure they're okay. I feel a soft hand on my back and I remember the reason--Genevieve. Sparring with her, fucking her keeps me distracted and it makes me a bastard, but I need the calm again.

I turn around, roughly cupping her cheeks and lift her face to me.

"Let Kenzie sleep by Rochelle tonight. Come home with me."

"Machlin..." She puts her hand over mine and I see the battle in her gaze. "What are we doing? What is this?"

"I don't know but let's just keep doing it."

"You're using me to avoid talking about your sister," she says, arching an eyebrow.

"Yes."

Her eyes widen at my honesty.

"Wow, not even going to try and deny it, huh?"

"I promised you no more secrets," I whisper.

I kick myself for reminding her of that. I am still keeping a secret from her: that fucking plane ride. She's going to really hate me this time. I can't let her go yet. I need to keep her a little longer, keep her from making myself go crazy and feel things, feel the past five years come crashing down on me like it's threatening to.

She closes her eyes and nods.

"I...it's only fair since I might have used you the other day," she says softly.

"Your mother?"

She nods again and I lift her face, forcing her to look at me.

"Stay with me tonight, let's forget together. Just for tonight."

I open my eyes and feel a warm spot on my chest. I look down and realize Genevieve is there, the night coming back to me. Crashing through the front door of my house and burying myself inside her all night. The foyer, the shower, the couch and then finally in bed. I remember her trying to escape in the middle of the night and I pulled her back, burying myself inside her again, falling asleep still there.

She stirs from my chest and I kiss her forehead, pushing aside her hair.

"Do you want breakfast?" I whisper.

"Mmm hmm. I can make us some. And coffee--like, an IV of coffee," she sighs.

I laugh and sit up a little pushing her chin to look at me. We've always done the frantic, quick, raw fuck but last night was different. It *felt* different. We slept a whole night together for fucks sake. I don't think I've spent the night with a woman in ten years.

"I...last night, Genny--"

"Don't, Machlin. We were both two consenting adults, we did nothing wrong. I agreed to come back here of my own free will and...last night was amazing. We can just leave it at that, okay?"

I can see the war in her gaze. She doesn't want to give this up, but neither do I. Can I handle taking care of two more people, though? I'm already drowning on the inside and two more people might just sink me for good. I don't want to take everyone else down with me.

"I..."

"I think we both need to figure out our shit before this could ever be something, Machlin. I'm not stupid, I know what this is...an escape. I use you just as much as you use me. I can't...deal with things sometimes, I don't know how or maybe I just don't want to. You erase that for me. I don't know why, and it pisses me off to be honest. You hurt me and I don't want you to be the one to fix me. I'm not making any sense right now," she says, pulling the sheet up to cover her bare breasts.

"You are making sense and I'm sorry I hurt you. What I said to you the first time we met..." I shake my head. "I like riling you up, I don't know why, but I do. That night though, that was for the undercover boss routine. I had to push you away from Machlin and towards Adam. I had to make you think I was a bastard, that there could never be something between us so you would look at Adam like that. I needed you to give him your trust for it to work."

She nods and shakes her head.

"I see it now. I don't like it and it still pisses me off, but I understand it."

"Genevieve, you're a stronger person than I ever will be for admitting all of this. You recognize your faults and you put them out there and I...don't know how to do that, I don't want to do that, I *can't* do that."

She cups my face and studies me.

"Why not?"

"I just can't, okay?"

"Mac, you're human, you're not a robot. You're allowed to have feelings."

"Not in my position."

"Talk to me. Just let it out," she pushes.

"Stop pushing me, Genevieve. You won't like what you find. This is who I am and I'm not gonna change."

"Why?"

"Because people count on me, dammit! A whole god damn company counts on me to not fuck up! People need this job to put food on their table, to provide for their family and it's on my shoulders! I have four people that look to me for guidance, for answers, for advice! My father left *me* with that responsibility! I am to take care of them as he would have. Him and my mother busted their asses for us, and they still were killed, dammit! Left us all shattered and I didn't have time to stop and feel sorry for myself! I don't have time to do that because I have to make sure everyone else doesn't feel the pain! I need to be the one to take it all away, I need to..."

I trail off, smacking my glass of water off the nightstand and burying my face in my hands. Everything comes barreling towards me--the funeral, the phone call about their car accident, holding my sisters at night, the sound of

197

their cries, pulling my brother out of the bar after another drunken night mourning our parents. Pulling Valentina to sit on her bed because she would collapse on her bedroom floor, crying uncontrollably. Our parents were our world and then it was shattered, and I never got to deal with that.

I start to cry, angry hurt tears as I smack my lamp to the floor, the bulb shattering. I get to my feet and stomp to my desk, tossing all the papers off, throwing my paper weight across the room. I wind back and punch my fist through the wall; punch after punch and finally my body surrenders, the anger leaving and the grief strangling me. I let out a loud sob as I drop to the floor, my head in between my legs, my hands behind my neck.

I never asked for this responsibility. I started Saddler Enterprises because I wanted to provide for my family so they would never feel the way they felt when they were helpless and poor, but I never thought I would do it without my father by my side. I thought he would be here, helping me, guiding me, proud of me and then someday adding a wife and a child to pass this legacy down to. I cry as I mourn the loss of my parents but the loss of my other dreams. Dreams I can't have because I need to focus on everyone else and not myself.

"Machlin..."

Then her voice pulls me out. Her hand is on my bare back and her soft lips touch my shoulder.

I look up, tears streaming down her own face as she cups my cheeks and I lean into her touch.

"I'm sorry..." I sob. "I'm so, so sorry."

She crawls forward and pulls my head against her chest as I wrap my arms around her, burying my face against her skin and continue to cry.

"You have nothing to be sorry for. Shhh, you have *nothing* to be sorry for."

I bring my face up, looking into her eyes and I stand, lifting her with me as I walk us to the bed. I drop her gently to the mattress and line my shaft up with her entrance and slowly push inside her. The anger, the sadness evaporating from my body, like a different person. Those problems are not mine, they belong to someone else.

"My problems don't exist when I'm inside you. All I feel is...bliss."

"Machlin, you're describing a drug...an addiction."

"I'm describing you, Genny. What I feel when I'm with *you*."

She sighs as she cups my cheeks again.

"Machlin, you can't keep running from this, using me to--"

"Please, Genny. Just for tonight."

We stare at each other, my body slowly moving as she silently nods, and I pick up my pace. Our foreheads touch as our eyes stay locked and her mouth starts to open as I move a little faster, my thrusts harder. I softly kiss her lips as she wraps her hands around my back, gripping my skin as I feel her start to tense.

This is different. This isn't our angry fuck this is...*making love*. I'm using her to ease my pain but something else is forming in its place. It's not an empty bliss, a momentary block of responsibilities, it's...warm, and different. A feeling I've never felt before.

I hear Genevieve's soft gasp and look down, a small smile on her lips and I release myself inside her, realizing right now that I'm falling in love with Genevieve Langston.

Chapter 19
Machlin

I walk into the office and immediately spot a big pile of papers on my desk. I'm always so organized and I didn't leave this here last night when I left. The feeling of dread overpowers me, and I walk over glancing at the pile.

There is a hand-written note on the top and I furrow my brows.

She's the one you wanted this whole time.

I push the note away and look through the papers. There are fifteen pairs of closing documents, all with Whitney Roark on them. There are two sets of documents for each closing, the housing prices different from the original. I smile knowing that we have Jeremy where we want him but then I stop, realizing Genevieve's name is also there. All fifteen of them.

"What the fuck," I whisper.

I sit at my desk, dropping my briefcase on the floor as I go through each document, comparing all the numbers.

Shit. Shit. Shit.

I groan, rubbing my hand down my face and pick up my cell phone, knowing I have to confront Genevieve about this before I bring it to Elijah's attention. I need to give her the benefit of the doubt.

She picks up on the first ring out of breath.

"What's up? I'm about to get in the elevator now, sorry I'm late. Kenzie just--"

"It's okay, Genn. Just come straight to my office please."

I hang up before she answers and I stand, pacing around my office, trying like hell to control myself. I know she would never steal from the company. She's a reliable woman, she's honest and hard-working but what if Jeremy got to her, just like he got to Whitney Roark? Elijah looked her up and she's also a single mother. Maybe that's his ploy; preying on the weak? Could she have known but was too scared to say anything?

We've been different the past few days after my breakdown at the house. We haven't talked about it, but we also haven't communicated in more than a professional manner. She doesn't sass me, and I don't tell her that I want to bend her over my desk. I haven't touched her since, and she looks away, breaking eye contact every time I look at her. We both don't know how to navigate this. I've broken down and dealt with my feelings, but she still hasn't. She said it herself; we have to deal with our own shit before we can possibly start something with each other.

Have I dealt with my own shit, though? Destroying my room, crying and then forcing myself on Genevieve hardly seems like dealing with it. I sigh, running my hands through my hair as I hear a soft knock from behind me,

"Hey, you wanted to see me?"

Genevieve walks through my doorway and she has glasses on, her eyes are red and her hair is in a messy bun. She never has her hair up, and she never wears glasses.

"Are you okay?"

"I'm fine. I...just had a rough night. What's going on, it sounded like an emergency?" she asks, sitting down in the chair opposite my desk.

I want to know why she had a rough night so I can make it better, but I can sense the cold Genevieve and know if I push, I'll only make it worse.

"I am only going to ask you this once and you are going to answer me truthfully."

She looks up and crosses her arms over her chest.

"I'm always honest with you, Machlin. What is it?"

"Are you working with Jeremy on these closings to steal money from the company?"

Her jaw drops and she opens and closes her mouth a few times before she gets to her feet.

"I really hope this is a joke, Machlin," she snaps.

"Answer the question, Genevieve."

"Of course I'm not stealing money with Jeremy! How could you even ask that? You said you didn't think it was me when I asked you. Why the change?"

"Do these look familiar?" I ask, as I push the documents towards her.

She reaches for them and starts to sift through, gasping.

"Machlin, I swear, I've never seen this set before. What...where did you even get this? How...how did he change this?" she asks, in a whisper.

"Whitney Roark. She's been on every single one of these closings. He puts down the loan price for the bank higher than the price it actually sells for then pockets the difference." I say, slamming a paper down on my desk.

"How does the buyer not realize their mortgage is higher than it should be? If he puts a loan in for 300 but they only need 250 then their monthly mortgage would be at least $100 higher, no?" she asks with confusion.

"Look at the interest rate," I say, standing by my window, running my hand down my chin.

"So, she's been changing the loan amount and increasing the interest. They think the extra $100 is the interest and have no freaking clue. Jesus. He really thought this through. God, Whitney is such a good person, how could she do this?" she asks with a sigh.

"She's a single mother. My guess is Jeremy blackmailed her somehow. I have to nab him, but I don't know how to do that without her going down, too."

"Machlin, please don't. Please talk to her. I know what it's like doing this on my own, it's so hard. She may not have been given a choice," Genevieve pleads, putting her hand on my back.

I feel the jolt, her touch that I've missed these past few days.

"She may just be good at fooling people, Genevieve. Did you think of that?" I argue.

"Why are you slinging that attitude towards me? I didn't do anything."

"Because this is my company, Genevieve. I didn't ask for your opinion or how to go about this. I called you here to make sure you had nothing to do with it and you didn't, so thank you. You can leave now."

I whip back around and close my eyes, hating the tone I used with her, but my anger took over. My anger at someone manipulating my company, using it to gain their own sleazy money and me not figuring it out.

"You're angry at yourself, not me. I'll be in my office awaiting your apology," she snaps.

I hear her heels clacking on my floor then my office door opening and then slamming, rattling a picture frame on my wall. When she's right, she's right. I am angry at myself. Angry for not figuring this out, angry for breaking down in front of her the other night, angry at not being able to juggle all these different balls and bring her and Kenzie into the mix. I want them both there dammit, but I don't know if I'm strong enough yet. I'm trying, I'm really trying.

I sit back down in my chair and reach for my cellphone as a knock on my door stops me.

"What the hell did you do to Genevieve?" my brother asks.

"Nothing. I asked her if she was involved in this shit and she wasn't."

I toss the papers to the other side of the desk and watch his face as he reads them.

"Well hell, this fucker. We got him, Mac. I'll bring all this to the lawyer and--"

"I want to speak to the woman, Whitney. I don't want her to be reprimanded if she was a victim in all this."

Elijah eyes me and nods as he takes out his cell phone.

"When?"

"As soon as possible."

He nods as he presses a few buttons on his phone and then looks up at me.

"I'll have her here by today."

I nod and look back down at my desk, twirling my phone around the dark mahogany.

"And Genevieve?" Elijah asks.

"What about her?"

"Are you going to talk with her? She was upset and crying. Are you guys--"

"Colleagues, Elijah. We are colleagues."

"Right, just colleagues. Then why is your jaw flexing like that?"

"Because she drives me up a fucking wall!"

"Easy, why are you so angry?"

"Because she makes me like this, dammit."

"Why do you let her get to you then, if you don't even like her?"

"Because I do, Elijah! I love her!"

He opens his mouth to argue more but then stops, his lips forming into a smile.

"I never thought I'd see the day. Are you going to tell her, or just brood in here?"

"I can't, Elijah. I can't do a goddamn thing about it because I lied about the plane ride and I have to worry about everyone else. I can't take care of all of you and still have enough love to give to Kenzie and Genny. They deserve someone that can give them everything they have, not an afterthought," I grumble.

"Worry about who?"

"You! Val, Rochelle, Dax...the people of the company...everyone!"

He laughs and shakes his head, slapping me on the back of my head.

"What the fuck, Elijah!"

"Machlin, I'm a grown ass man and Valentina is a grown woman, hell Rochelle is too! We don't need you to look out for us, we look out for *each other*...all of us, *together*. Now, I know dad must have said things in his letter to you. We all got them, and I can only guess what he said in yours, but we're older now, Mac. This company is run by *both* of us. I have just as much a burden on my shoulders as you do, so don't think you need to take all the weight. Rochelle handles herself well on Startups, she is a Saddler after all. You forget we all have the same blood, brother. We're hard fucking workers, we're hustlers and we do it as a *family*. Yes, you're the oldest and you've had to take the reins for a while, but mom and dad taught us well and so have you. Now it's time to let us all handle ourselves and be there if we need you. Don't take our troubles from us and make them your own."

"But Val--"

"Val is...going to deal with things for the rest of her life, Machlin. There are...things she'll discuss with you when she's ready but there is only so much *we* can do for her. We all handle things differently and right now, focus on *your* part of the business and *your* life. You're a great brother and I see how you are with Kenzie. You would be an amazing dad, an amazing partner but you just have to let yourself. The only one standing in the way of all that is you. Don't put other people to blame for something that only *you* can fix. When all of us get our happy ending, where will you be, brother?"

I eye my brother and give him a small smile, patting him on the back.

"How did that bitch Gretchen snatch a guy like you, huh?" I laugh.

"Not you too. That's going to be your future sister-in-law and my wife. You can't talk about her like that," he rages.

"If we're dishing out advice now, mind if I take a crack at it?" I ask.

"I doubt I have a choice, asshole."

"Ditch Gretchen, Elijah. She's nothing but trouble and only after your money. You'll thank me one day when you find a woman worth it. A woman that's with you just for you, not for what you can buy her."

"Like I said, people deal with things differently. Thank you for the advice, but I'm going to politely decline that one."

I shrug and sit back down in my chair.

"Suit yourself."

He walks towards my door and then turns around.

"Val texted by the way. She'll be home tomorrow morning."

I nod and watch him leave as I glance back down at the picture on my desk, reaching for it and running my thumb along my parents faces. No matter the hardships they went through, they always had those smiles on their faces. I think back to the years and wonder when I ever looked as happy as they did, that genuine ear to ear smile and my mind goes to the plane.

Sitting with Genevieve and Kenzie--although she was sad and broken--I remember seeing her face and that's where it all started. The sunshine on the dark day, like a breath of fresh air after being suffocated. Kenzie cuddling up to me on that place, on the couch, the lost look in her eyes, the one that mirrored my own, disappearing when I was with her and Genn.

They were my happy place. I open my top drawer and pick out the strip of pictures we took at the fair. Our tongues hanging out in one, kissy faces in the other and my favorite of all three--Kenzie smiling while Genn and I smush her cheeks with a kiss. Kenzie's little hands are cupping our cheeks and I can't help the smile that forms on my own face. My brother's words playing in my mind. When they all find their forever, I'll be all alone.

Chapter 20
Genevieve

I open the door to my house and am greeted by Rochelle and a woman that looks exactly like her only with Elijah's blue eyes, instead of Rochelle's brown.

"Oh honey, you look like shit," Rochelle coos, bringing me in for a hug.

I squeeze her and try to laugh but it turns into a soft sob and she squeezes my shoulder. I keep the tears at bay though as she turns to the woman.

"Genn, this is my sister, Valentina. She's home for a while, hope you don't mind that I brought her. I really didn't have a choice," she says, nodding to Valentina.

"Rude!" Valentina says, slapping Rochelle's arm. "In my defense, she basically kidnapped me. I didn't know I was crashing a girl's night. It's nice to meet you, Genevieve," Valentina laughs while shaking my hand.

"You didn't. Don't even worry about it, you're always welcome. It's nice to meet you, too. I have to be honest, you do look like Elijah, but I swear you could pass for twins with Rochelle."

Valentina nods and waves her hand.

"I used to be blonde, then you wouldn't say that."

"Really? What made you dye it?"

"I...just needed a change," Valentina says, with a sad smile. "How about wine?"

She lifts the bottle and I nod, letting them both through the doorway.

"So why are we kicking my brother's ass? I mean there is a long list of reasons, I'm sure, but why are you crying? Let's start with that one," Rochelle says, coming to sit at the kitchen island.

Before I can open my mouth, I hear Kenzie crying upstairs and take them two at a time, rushing to her side.

"Mama! Mama!" she cries.

"Shhh, Kenzie baby, Genny is here. I'm here, baby, it's okay," I soothe, pulling her in for a hug.

She grips me, hugging me tight to her body as she cries into my shirt.

"Miss Mama...m-miss...M-Mama," she sobs.

I run my hand down her hair and kiss her head, rocking her in bed with me, singing the song that Tonya used to sing to her at night. I don't know how to make this stop for her, make her get a good night's sleep without missing Tonya. I feel myself start to cry, break down like I did all day today and everything crashes down on me.

I'm letting her down: Kenzie, Tonya, my mother...everyone. I can't even help myself. Stumbling into bed with Machlin Saddler, knowing full well I would hurt myself in the end, but I didn't care. I used the temporary relief and now I'm paying for it. I could only go so long ignoring all this hurt.

"Oh baby, it's okay," I sob now, holding Kenzie as I cry. "Kenzie is my baby. I love her like crazy. Baby, baby, I love her like crazy. One, two, three, Mackenzie and me. One, two, three, my baby and me."

I break on the last line of the song and feel a hand on my back as I lean into it, holding Kenzie to my chest.

"It's okay...we're here, Genn. It's okay," Rochelle soothes.

I nod, kissing Kenzie as I rock us, Rochelle gripping me tight and I hear Kenzie's sobs slowly quiet down. Soon her cries turn into snores and I lean her back, tucking the blanket up to her chin. I kiss her cheek, seeing one of my tears spill onto her soft skin and I wipe it off.

"I love you, baby," I whisper.

I stand and see Valentina wiping her eyes from the doorway. Rochelle is behind me, her hand on my back guides me downstairs.

"Is this still happening every night?" Rochelle asks, pushing a glass of wine to me.

Valentina takes a sip and turns to look out the window, sniffling.

"I'm so sorry, I didn't mean to make this such a cryfest," I laugh, wiping at my eyes.

Valentina turns, her eyes red and she gives me a smile.

"No, no it's okay. I'm a mess on my own without all this. It's not your fault."

Rochelle eyes her and Valentina swats her worry away again.

"But yeah, every night. Most nights I just sleep with her because I end up in her bed anyway. I don't know what to do. I...I'm so...lost," I say, my voice defeated.

211

"We need to get your mother help, Genn. No matter what she says, we need to check her into a place that she can't check herself out of and she needs to get better. I'll handle that, you just focus on Kenzie, okay?" Rochelle says, putting her hand on my shoulder.

"Okay, that I can do."

I take a long sip from my wine glass and Valentina and Rochelle glance at each other.

"What?" I ask.

"My brother...we had a family meeting the other night. He's got a lot of guilt weighing him down and put a lot of responsibility on himself that he didn't need to. I know he's an asshole, Genn, but all I ask is you give him one more chance. He's different with you and he admitted it to us...all of us. He never does that, talk about himself. It was...weird but good, if that makes sense."

I nod and take another sip, then put my glass down. I remember when he broke down in front of me at his house, the stresses he admitted to feeling for his siblings and I'm happy he's opened up to all of them, he needed that.

"Listen, Rochelle. We...our relationship wasn't what I would call a healthy one. We fought, we used each other, and we were just physical."

"Genevieve, I'm sorry, but if you believe that then you are delusional. Yes, you fought, yes you fuck, but come on. You can't tell me that what you felt for him was nothing more than physical. I saw the way you guys looked at each other."

"Like we wanted to rip each other's heads off? Or clothes? Because it was always a mix of both to be honest," I scoff.

"Okay, yes, a little of both, but everyone's relationship is different. You would never hurt each other, that was the difference. Your fighting was just...foreplay," she says, with a shrug.

"Okay, if I can chime in here for just a second, being an outside party and all," Valentina says, holding up her finger. "We have my brother, your friend, Kenzie, your mom...is there anything else going on? We're here to help, so tell us everything."

I look at her and really try to narrow down the question. I feel like it's a mix of everything. I didn't really get to mourn Tonya because I got thrust into being a mom. I threw myself into Kenzie and my new job, worrying about my mother in the only spare moments I got. Then there was Machlin and the feelings I had when I was with him; fighting him, kissing him, *being* with him. Everything else faded away when I was with him and thinking I could never have that happiness anymore was my breaking point.

"A little of everything," I say softly. "But feeling like things were finally at the end with your brother maybe pushed it all over the edge."

"Why are they over? I mean you got over the undercover boss thing, right?" Rochelle asks.

I nod and she keeps going.

"Got over the whole possibly accusing you of working with Jeremy, right?"

I shrug my shoulders.

"I mean, I guess. That kind of hurt, but whatever."

"So, is this because of the whole plane guy thing?"

I start to shrug but stop.

"Wait, plane guy thing? What plane guy thing?"

Rochelle opens her mouth and then shuts it, closing her eyes and letting out a sigh.

"Oh, fuck me. This is...not about plane guy, is it?"

Valentina smacks the back of Rochelle's head and I sit up a little straighter.

"Plane guy? MJ plane guy? What about him?"

"He um...I..."

I drop my wine glass to the table and gasp, putting all these pieces together and once again, feeling like a goddamn idiot.

"Machlin is...was...plane guy. Machlin was MJ...this whole time he...was Adam and MJ and...my God, is there something wrong with me? Three men! All three fucking men and I didn't have a clue! Jesus Christ," I snap, getting to my feet.

"Genn, it's understandable, I mean you were a wreck on the plane, and you've been dealing with a lot of shit. I mean I didn't even recognize him as Adam at first! I was hitting on him for fucks sake!" Rochelle says, getting to her feet too.

"I'm...so stupid. All this time... I need to talk to him. Stay here with Kenzie, I need to go talk to him," I say, brushing past the two of them.

"Genevieve, you shouldn't talk to him angry like this. Take the night and first thing tomorrow--"

"No." I cut off Valentina's plea. "I need to go now. I need my anger because tomorrow he'll make me forget. This is what he does! He makes me forget all the troubles in my life and I need him to keep doing it! I can't continue on like this. I need to face everything. I need to fucking break down so I can pick myself up. I need to end this. Please...stay with Kenzie," I beg.

Rochelle sighs as does Valentina and they both nod.

"You shouldn't drive though. I'll stay with Kenzie since she knows me in case she wakes up. Val will drive you."

I nod as I walk towards the front of my house, throw on my sneakers and walk out towards Rochelle's car. We take the ride in silence until we're outside Machlin's house and Valentina puts her hand on my knee.

"Genevieve, I know I don't know you, but I do know what being broken does to a person. I admire you for everything that is on your plate--how you juggle it all--even though you think you don't. Believe me when I say, things do not just go away, but you learn to live with them the best you can. If my brother makes any of that better for you, helps you live a little easier with it, don't let him go. Hold onto him with everything you have."

Her voice breaks and I nod, squeezing her hand.

"I'll be back in a little, okay?"

She nods as I get out, her words softening me a little bit. I remember what Machlin said about her, how she runs away from their town because her heart was shattered. I don't want to make the same mistake, but I also don't want to start a life with a liar, with a man who only saw pity when he looked at me. I need to be strong, stand my ground by myself and cut Machlin out...for good.

Chapter 21
Genevieve

I knock on Machlin's front door, tapping my foot, waiting for him to open it. After a few seconds he opens the door, his hair a mess with his glasses on and a shocked expression on that gorgeous face.

"Genevieve? What are you doing here?"

"Can I come in? We have something to talk about."

My voice is hard and he takes notice. His jaw flexes into that expression I love--when he's gearing up for a fight with me. He nods, letting me inside and shuts the door. When he turns around, his body in shorts and a t-shirt is my kryptonite, but I push past the desire to forget--to lose myself with him--and remember why I'm here.

"Were you the man from the plane? MJ?"

He exhales, running his hand down the stubble on his face. It's only been a day since I've walked out of his office, waiting patiently for an apology that never came. He looks miserable, like he hasn't showered or groomed himself in weeks.

"Yes."

"We said no more lies! *You* said no more lies, dammit! How could you? There were so many opportunities for you to tell me!"

"I didn't lie, I just...didn't relay all the information. I'm sorry, okay? I just knew this is what would happen, and I didn't want to deal with it."

"No, you didn't want to deal with it, just like you don't want to deal with anything!"

"You're any different?" he scoffs.

"I admitted it, Mac! I *can't* deal with shit, I run away from it and jump right to you, but at least I don't lie!"

"Which me?" he says, with a smug smirk.

"What the hell is so funny?"

"You don't think it's crazy? I mean I don't believe in fate and all that shit but all three men you fell for were me! I mean you seemed to be mighty thirsty with all the problems you were trying to hide behind, but I doubt any man would have sufficed. You had plenty to choose from in the office all those months but held out for me."

I let out a sarcastic laugh and poke his chest. "I'm taking vacation! Fuck the policy, I'm not answering my phone and when I get back, I'm not catching up on my work! I can't believe you think this is some big joke!" I say, turning towards his front door, trying hard as Hell to hold back the tears.

"Genny--"

I whip around and point my finger at him.

"You know what sucks? I fell hard for MJ because of how sweet he was with Kenzie and how refreshing and positive he was. I fell for Adam because he listened to me, opened up to me and was a nice person, but you--" I seethe, poking his chest. "I just like you because you're a good fuck. I could see myself with a man like MJ or Adam, but *you* sure as Hell don't deserve me!"

I turn and walk towards the door again, wiping at my stubborn tears.

"Genny--"

"Stop calling me that!"

"Okay, okay," he says lifting his hands in defense. "I get you're mad. I'm making it worse and I'm being a dick. But I just can't do this forever thing with you. You need someone other than me. I'm sorry if I made you think otherwise."

I let out a sarcastic laugh again, wiping my eyes and turning towards him.

"Do me a favor? Fuck yourself. You're such an asshole and not *once* did I ever see a forever thing with *you*, Machlin Saddler. It would require you to pull your head out of your ass and we all know that's *never* going to happen. I'm taking a vacation and you'll get my two weeks notice. If you black ball me in Tucson, I swear I'll go to HR and claim sexual harassment. God knows it's true anyway," I declare, turning on my heel.

"Genevieve, you wouldn't," Machlin says, grabbing my arm.

I spin around and pull my arm free, pinning him with my stare.

"Try me!"

"Is that...that's what you think I did? Harassed you? Genn-- Genevieve, I never meant--"

"You play fair and so will I. It was all mutual, Machlin and I never would claim otherwise. But if you don't allow me to leave and find a new job, then that's messing with Kenzie's life too and I won't have that. I'll be gone for the weekend, make the right decision."

I reach for the knob, but his hand comes down on top of mine, stopping me...again.

"Please forgive me, Genevieve. I didn't want you to think I only gave you the job because I saw how broken you were on that plane," he whispers.

"Didn't you?" I yell turning around. "Didn't you feel so bad for the girl that just buried her best friend? That now had to take care of a child that reminded her every damn day of what she lost? With no fucking family except an alcoholic mother that barely keeps herself alive and doesn't really give a shit about her? Try and tell me that isn't the reason!" I yell, tears streaming down my face.

"So what if it was!" he yells back. "At first it was. I felt bad, Genevieve. I may be a dick, but I have a heart! I saw you struggling and wanted to do something nice and in case you forgot, I know what it's like to lose someone you love! Two in fact!"

I open my mouth and close it, shaking my head.

"Machlin, I--"

"Let me finish," he says through clenched teeth.

I clench my own, hating his tone and the anger coming off his body. *I* should be mad at *him,* not the other way around!

"I don't just go hiring people off the street, Genny. Elijah looked into you and we called your old job in New York. We spoke to your professors and we called references. Yes, initially I did it because I felt sorry for you, but it was also helping *me* out. Jeremy was a piece of shit and I saw a future with you here at Saddler Enterprises. I saw you

219

taking his place and running the entire floor as my CFO. Don't for a second get that twisted, Genevieve Langston. I may have handed you my card out of pity but as soon as you stepped into *my* building, you stayed because you earned it. If you want to leave, I won't stop you. I shouldn't have gotten involved with you, that was my own fault for not being able to control my desires. As far as work is concerned, I will leave you be if you choose to stay. I will make sure our time together is limited as much as possible."

I'm dumbfounded, frozen into place as he eyes me, looking for a reaction. He doesn't understand it, and as much as admitting all of this is going to make me look like an idiotic fool, he won't get it unless I do.

"The fact that you can just turn this off is the problem. I can't, Machlin. Despite what I said, it wasn't just about sex for me. I saw glimpses of Adam and MJ in you and I want that--I want all of that--but you'll never be able to give that to me, you said it yourself."

"But you just said--"

"I know what I said but I was hurt. The truth is, I fell in love with you, Mac. You made me forget about all the shit in my life I couldn't control, and I thought that was a bad thing, but it wasn't. Maybe that's how our love works, everyone's is different. I helped you forget and you me. Yes, we have to solve problems and talk, but you made me *happy*. Even when I was fighting with you, I felt more alive than I have in a long, long time. So no, I can't just be in the same building as you, sit across from you at a meeting and have you look at me as if what we shared was nothing more than physical. You do, and that's fine, I can't change your mind, but I also can't change my own. I...Am I off or am I right?"

His facial expression doesn't change, he doesn't give me an answer and it kills me. Instead of lashing out, instead of grabbing his face and indulging in our explosive chemistry one last time, I nod silently and turn as he takes his hand off mine.

"Right, well I'm going to go. I'll be back to work on Monday."

I turn and leave and this time, he doesn't stop me and no matter how desperately I want to turn around and beg him to not let me go--I don't. I keep walking towards Valentina and when I get inside the car, she doesn't say a word as I bury my face in my hands and let the stubborn tears fall for the asshole I swore I would never give my heart to. A man I knew wouldn't cherish and protect it, but I gave it to him anyway.

I put my glasses on, foregoing my contacts because my eyes are practically closed and I don't feel like attempting to pry them open. I slept like fucking shit last night and don't even feel satisfaction for what's coming today like I thought I would. I'm finally nailing Jeremy red handed but I don't even care. She told me she loved me, and I fucking stood there like a god damn idiot.

I slam my hand on my desk and walk towards my office door, locking it behind me. I chain called Rochelle and she said if Genevieve isn't picking up my calls, then she doesn't want to talk to me, and I should be patient. It's been two days. I don't fucking know how to be patient.

I get in the back seat of my car as Michael drives us to the bank for the closing. My mind is reeling and my anger coming to the surface at Genevieve's ability to ignore me...Jeremy stealing from this company. It's slowly toppling over as Michael pulls up and I get out.

"Give me a half hour," I say to him.

He nods and I walk towards the entrance, ignoring the greetings I get as I walk inside. Jeremy is alone in the conference room, typing something on his phone as he paces the floor.

I walk in and shut the door behind me, as he jumps, looking up.

"M-Mr. Saddler, w-what are you doing here? Genevieve and I are--"

"Genevieve is no longer on closings with you, In fact, it's more like the other way around. You're fired, Jeremy."

I turn on my heel and go to open the door, but his words stop me.

"You're firing me? On what grounds?"

"You'll be finding out very soon," I say, whipping around. "No one fucking steals from *my* company because that means you're fucking with *my* family and I'll die before I ever let that happen," I say, through clenched teeth.

Jeremy's gaze darkens as the conference door opens and two police officers come in, reading Jeremy his rights.

"You were the intern, weren't you? I should have known. You'll pay for this, Machlin Saddler. Mark my words, you'll pay."

I shake my head at him as I motion for the officers to take him out and then sit in one of the chairs, composing myself. The vindication I thought I would feel, putting Jeremy where he belongs and giving him what he deserves, isn't there. I feel...empty and I know the only way to fill that is with the one woman that hates me.

Genevieve

I pack the last bag in the trunk of my car and walk towards the front, looking to the backseat at Kenzie and Valentina.

"Ready to go?" I ask.

"You know me, I'm always up for an adventure," Valentina says smiling.

"I literally don't think I've taken a vacation since--"
Rochelle stops talking from the front seat next to me and I
eye her.

"Since when?" I ask, pulling out of my driveway.

"Since Spain?" Valentina asks, with amusement.

"Shut the fu--zip it, Val," Rochelle growls.

"Don't tell me your BFF doesn't know about, *Rico Suave*,"
Valentina teases.

"Don't call him that! He's an as--donkey," Rochelle says,
turning towards the back seat, pointing at her sister.

"Hey, watch your mouth over there, *Princesa*," Valentina
chides.

"You have no idea what the hell you're talking about!"
Rochelle snaps.

Val and I are both silent and Rochelle lets out a breath.

"I'm sorry, I'm sorry. I just...you don't talk about Declan,
Val...don't make me talk about Rafa, okay?" she sighs.

"Okay, I get it. I'm sorry. I mean it wasn't a mutual
thing...the way you parted? I always thought it was?" Val
asks.

"Were you and Declan?"

"Fair enough. Let's not do this. It's about Genevieve and her
vacation and we're supposed to be having fun," Val
concedes.

"Thank you. But there is no way either of you are getting
away with not spilling the beans. You guys made me cut
myself open, it's only fair."

"Can we wait until we get to the cabin and have oh, I don't know...like six margaritas?" Rochelle says, with a smile.

Valentina and I both laugh as I continue to drive to Valentina's cabin on Big Lake, by the scenic White Mountains. Apparently, Rochelle said it was where Valentina escaped to after her break up with her ex-boyfriend, Declan.

It's a few hours drive which gives me time to think, which might not be a good thing. All I'm thinking about is Machlin: his words, my words, his lack of words, how things played out. I admitted to him that I loved him, and he said nothing, *did* nothing.

"Right up here on the left. Turn down the long drive," Valentina says.

I make the turn and drive the long path to a beautiful wooden cabin with floor to ceiling windows, overlooking the lake. There are two rocking chairs on the porch, and I cut the engine, getting out with a gasp.

"My God. This is beautiful, Valentina."

"Thanks. I uh...haven't been here in a while. It's..." She stops talking and swallows, looking out towards the lake. "Let me go on and unlock everything."

She walks ahead of us and I turn back to Rochelle.

"He was the love of her life. She's never been the same," Rochelle says, shaking her head. "They traveled the world together. She dropped out of High School to be with him. They lived together on his air force base and then he was deployed and poof! Done."

"He...he's still...alive, right?" I gulp.

"Yeah, he's fine. He just...broke her. I hope coming here wasn't a bad idea. When she volunteered her cabin, I didn't put two and two together until Elijah said something."

"I feel terrible now. Maybe we can rent something else?"

"No, it's okay. Maybe she needs this. Grab Kenzie and I'll grab our bags."

I open the back door for Kenzie and unbuckle her as she falls back asleep on my shoulder. Rochelle follows as we walk through the front door and hear sniffles from the kitchen. We both eye each other and she nods as I walk forward and see Valentina leaning over the counter, her shoulders bouncing.

"Val..." Rochelle says softly, putting her hand on her back.

"I'm fine, I'm fine. It's just...a lot coming back here. This...was where I got his letter and I...I just need a minute, okay? You guys make yourselves at home. This is fine, I promise," she says, with a strained smile, walking out towards the patio doors.

She opens them softly and steps out as she shuts them behind her.

"That's not just first love stuff, Rochelle. What the hell happened between them?" I ask, laying Kenzie on the living room couch.

"She doesn't talk about it. Elijah is the only one who knows the whole story and anytime I press him, he says it's not his to tell. I mean it's been almost twelve years and I still have no clue. I think she's taking it to the grave with her."

"God, I...it breaks my heart. Now I kind of get where Machlin was coming from, I guess. I wish I could help her and I just met her. I can't imagine how he must feel, thinking he's responsible for her and not knowing how to help."

I groan, realizing now that he did the same with me. Seeing me struggle on the plane, trying to help me out just like he does with everyone else. He didn't do it out of pity, he did it because he...*cared*. There really was no way of him moving me up, just to move me up.

I worked hard, I gained my clients trust all on my own. I worked my ass off during the day, put in so many hours out in the field, staging to perfection, finding the perfect homes for all my clients. There was no way any of that could have been set up. I'm a fool, I didn't even let him explain.

"You okay?" Rochelle asks.

"I'm...I need to talk to your brother. I made a big mistake, I--"

"Relax," Rochelle says putting a hand on my arm. "Take a day and think things through. When you go back, I want to make sure you're positive about what you want. Machlin isn't going anywhere, okay?"

I nod and she smiles at me.

"Now let's make some fucking margaritas. God knows we all need one!"

Chapter 23
Machlin

I feel a hard hit to the back of my head and lift it up quickly, looking from left to right.

"What happened? What...what's going on?" I ask, sleepily.

"Mac, what are you doing?" My youngest sister Dakota is staring at me with a scowl.

"Dax?" I ask, rubbing at my eyes. "What are you doing here?"

"Apparently, everyone is worried about you. I was coming home for spring break anyway but...what's happening?" She sits in the chair opposite my desk.

I look at my baby sister, her long brown hair, her button-down blouse and pencil skirt. She's wearing heels and I have to blink a few times to clear the fog.

"Dax, you look...old."

"Well, thanks. I am twenty, Mac. That's what happens to people. There's this thing called a birthday. Apparently, it's the day you were born and every year on your birthday you--"

"Okay, okay, I get it, smartass. I just meant that you look professional. Why are you so dressed?"

"I had an interview at Franklin High. They have an opening for a substitute biology teacher and since I'm graduating a year early, I figured I'd apply," she says, shrugging.

"You're not going to take the year and travel?" I ask, rubbing at my eyes again.

God, how long was I sleeping for?

"Nope. I want to just get my twenty-five years in and have nice early retirement to do that. I'm broke anyway, where the heck would I travel to?"

"Dax, I can pay for you to travel if that's what you want to do."

"Ahhh, now I see it. Is this what everyone is freaking out about? You taking care of all of us?"

"It's not a big deal, Dakota. If you want to travel I--"

"I don't want to travel, Machlin. I want to teach. That's what I went to school for, that's what I want to do. I have a plan and I'm not Valentina. I like things in order, but if I need money to travel, then guess what? I'll head up an after-school program, run one of the clubs to make a little extra cash or maybe get a roommate or something. I don't need your money and I don't need you to look after me. I just need my big brother. How did I do?" Dakota asks, with a smile.

"Not bad, peanut, not bad."

"Uhhh, when am I not going to be the peanut anymore? I'm almost legally allowed to drink!"

"You'll always be the peanut, but come here." I motion for her to come to my side of the desk.

She smiles and walks over, as I bring her in for a hug, kissing her forehead.

"I've missed you, Dax."

"I missed you too, Mac. Now tell me about Genn. I only met her briefly a few times, but I heard she gives you a run for your money." She sits on the edge of my desk.

"Oh, you did, huh? I'm not sure, she's...different."

"Isn't that the point? We don't want to find someone that is like everyone else, don't we want someone different? That's what makes them special, no?"

"You obviously got your philosophical talents from Elijah. Did you guys practice these speeches together or something?" I laugh.

I remember when Dakota was younger, so many nights sneaking into my bed, asking about our parents. She was fifteen, not too young to not remember them, but all the memories of us when we were younger. She liked to hear stories of her childhood, stories of mom and dad when they were younger and when it was only Elijah, Val and me and things were tight. She always said she liked to hear their obstacles because it made her grateful for everything she has now. She was always an old soul, more mature than all of us combined. Looking at her now--sitting right across from me--I realize that she's right. She really doesn't need me...none of them do.

"You're right," I say softly. "That is what you should look for. Genevieve is...strong and feisty. She doesn't have it all together but she sure as hell pretends that she does. She's...selfless..."

"Like you," Dakota finishes, nodding to me. "You're built for each other, then. Always taking care of other people, maybe that's why you're drawn together. You just needed each other...not anything else. You feel the weight of everything--the company, all of us, our parents. Maybe you were drawn to Genevieve because she just wanted *you* and you her."

I laugh, shaking my head at my sister and pull her to me, kissing the top of her head.

"Dakota Saddler, when the hell did you grow up?" I smile.

A loud bang from the hallway sounds and I immediately push Dakota behind me.

"What was that?" she asks in a panicked whisper.

"Get under my desk and don't move until I come and get you," I demand.

A gun. That was a fucking gunshot.

I walk towards my door slowly but stop in my tracks when Jeremy walks through my door aiming a gun at me.

"How the hell did you get in here with that? And why are you out of police custody?' I ask, putting my hands above my head.

"I have more friends than just Whitney Roark, Mr. Saddler. You should have done your research better," he seethes.

I knew this guy was bad news. I should have listened to my instincts and filed a restraining order. When I went to confront Whitney, she told me about his violent past and that he was threatening her, blackmailing her into going along with this. I should have known he was a loose cannon...had someone on him if he posted bail.

"I'm not going to jail, Mr. Saddler. You're going to burn all the information you think you found on me, recant all your statements and I am going to be set free. Do we understand each other?"

"Jeremy, there are security cameras throughout the whole building. Even if I let you go, you still brought a gun to this building with the intention of--"

"Shut up!" he yells, firing off a bullet to the wall behind me.

I flinch as I hear a yelp from underneath my desk and close my eyes.

"Who's that?" he asks, pointing the gun to the desk.

"It's no one. Please, Jeremy, let's settle this. Just me and you and leave everyone else out of it."

"Ms. Langston was in on it, too, but I know that's not her down there."

My blood runs cold at the mention of Genevieve and I remember the shot that was fired off in the hallway. She still won't answer my calls, I have no idea where she is.

"Jeremy...where is Genevieve?" I ask slowly, my heart pumping in my chest.

He gives me a malicious smile and I swear I want to throw up. If he...I can't think about it because I'll kill him. I will end his sorry ass and go to jail or end up dead myself.

"She's not a problem."

I close my eyes and grit my teeth, knowing that this won't end if I surrender. He's a fucking psycho and he'll put a bullet in me and Dakota and God knows who else. I hope someone has called 911, but I don't know how much time I have to work with. We could all be dead by the time they get here.

I look up at the ceiling, whispering to my parents asking for their protection and anything they could possibly do, God

232

or some type of higher power because my choices are slim. I look back at Jeremy and charge, tackling him to the ground but not before I hear a shot and a sharp pain ripping through my ribs.

"Machlin!"

My sister's voice is distant and then I hear my fathers...

Genevieve

"I'm just going to lay down right here on the floor, and you just pour all that coffee in my mouth," Rochelle groans, laying down on the kitchen floor.

I laugh and shake my head as Kenzie starts laughing too.

"I told you to stop drinking, you were shit faced. You started speaking Spanish," I laugh.

"I didn't," she groans. "I don't even know spanish! All I know is curses, dirty words and how to say I want you to fu--"

I lift my hand to stop her and laugh harder.

"Oh, we know, believe me we know. I found out more about you last night than I ever want to know."

"I'm staying right here all day. Seriously, just toss some eggs in my mouth from here like they do at those Hibachi places and let me go back to sleep."

I laugh as I shut the stove, plating the eggs and bacon and cutting some up for Kenzie.

"Ya know...you haven't mentioned your fuckadex in awhile..."

"I'm...taking a little break," Rochelle sighs.

"Break, huh?"

"Don't analyze me, Genn, I'm too hungover to be analyzed. That's the beauty about being single. When I'm sick of people's bullshit, I don't have to see them. I'm doing me for a while...literally. I lay myself better than half these pansy asses anyway."

"Not better than Rafa, though."

Rochelle snaps her head up and looks at me.

"Anything you remember from last night...forget, especially about him. *Hijo de puta...*" she whispers.

She lays back down, shaking her head as I toss a piece of bacon at her.

"Thought you'd be used to meat slapping you in the face," I laugh.

Rochelle scoffs and takes a big bite, pointing the piece of bacon at me.

"That was freaking good, Genevieve Langston. I knew I liked you!"

"There's been a shooting," Valentina yells, running into the kitchen. "At the office! Jeremy...Machlin..." She starts to cry and my heart stops beating as Rochelle scrambles to her feet.

"Is...is he okay?" I whisper.

"Val..." Rochelle starts to cry and put her hand over her mouth.

"We have to go. Machlin's in the hospital. It's bad…it's so bad."

I feel numb. I walk towards Kenzie in the highchair and lift her out. I don't even realize I walked down the stairs until I'm already in my car, driving back to town. Rochelle is crying in the front seat next to me, Valentina in the back and Kenzie is sleeping, thank God. I can't even cry because this isn't real.

Machlin is fine and this is all a big misunderstanding. Everything is going to be fine. I'm going to see him and apologize, and we'll move on like a family and everything will be fine. Except it's not…I know deep down in my heart everything is not okay, and the tears start to form. My safe place, my salvation when all the world is crumbling…he's not here to take it all away…he may never be again.

Chapter 24
Genevieve

I run down the hall of the hospital with Kenzie in my arms, Rochelle and Valentina in front of me. We all stop in front of the desk, rattling off Machlin's name and then rush to the elevators for the 3rd floor. Dakota and Elijah are there, pacing the hallway and they look up at us.

"How is he?" Valentina rushes to say.

"In surgery. It was...God it was so scary," Dakota says, as she starts to cry.

Valentina pulls her into a hug as they both cry and Rochelle walks over to Elijah.

"What the fuck happened?" she asks, wiping her eyes.

"Jeremy came into the office with a gun. Shot a blank in the hallway and went to Machlin. I was out at lunch, Dakota was there..."

"Dakota, Jesus Christ," Rochelle says, running her hand down Dakota's back. "What happened?"

"I w-went to talk to him about everything. We w-were in his office and that g-guy came in. Mac made me d-duck under the desk but then he s-shot one off the wall and I don't know. Mac c-charged at him I guess but I heard him y-yell and got up and Mac was on top of him. T-there was s-so much blood," Dakota cries.

My eyes start to water, and I hold in a cry with my hand over my mouth, careful not to startle Kenzie.

"Is...is he going to be okay?" I whisper.

They all look at me with sad eyes and I can't hold my cry in, shaking my head and turning away. I walk towards the chairs and sit down on one, Kenzie in my lap as I silently cry into her hair.

Me walking away from him can't be the last thing between us, it just can't.

Rochelle walks over, running her hand down my hair and leans my head on her shoulder.

"Y-you know he will be okay, Genn. He n-needs to be okay because whos g-going to f-fight with you," Rochelle stutters through her tears.

She gives me a small smile and I let out a cry-laugh, wiping at my own.

"He will be. He has to be."

Machlin

I try to open my eyes but they're heavy, like fucking lead weights and I try harder. I get one open, then struggle with the other as I slowly register where I am, the blurriness subsiding. I hear low beeps in the background and see the white walls and smell the sterilization.

Hospital. I'm in the hospital.

"You really can't ever back down from playing the hero, can you?" asks a female voice from my side.

I glance up and see Valentina and open my mouth to speak but my throat is so dry. She hands me a cup of water and puts it to my lips as I take a small sip.

"Is..." I clear my throat again as I remember what happened. "Is Dakota okay? Genny? Elijah? Rochelle?"

I sound like a 90-year-old smoker and my body aches with just the simple movements of talking.

"Everyone is fine. You scared the shit out of all of us, ya know? What were you thinking charging at that psycho like that?"

"I thought he...shot Genevieve. He would've...shot Dax," I say, wincing.

"Okay, stop talking and just listen because I'm only saying this once. There are things that happen in your life, Machlin, things that you have no control over. Things that you are going to do, mistakes that you are going to make and sometimes you are going to regret them for the rest of your life."

I watch as she tries to keep her emotions in check, but I know my sister. She's not just talking about me. I open my mouth to speak but she puts up her hand.

"I'm not finished."

I nod and let her continue.

"Do not let Genevieve Langston walking away be one of those things. That girl loves you and I know you feel the same. Kenzie..." Valentina stops, looking to the ceiling and her bottom lip quivers.

I slowly move my hand to cup hers on my bed and give her a soft squeeze.

"Kenzie deserves to have two people that love her and...you deserve to know what that feels like. You deserve to have someone love you as much as you love us all, okay? Promise me, Machlin," Val says, a lone tear dripping down her cheek.

"Val..."

"I'm fine, okay...just...promise me, you won't let them go."

I nod and she leans forward, kissing my forehead.

"I love you, brother. I'm happy you're okay."

"I love you, too. Where is the rest of the squad?"

"Elijah, Rochelle and Dax went to get some coffee. Genn headed home with Kenzie. She's been here in and out as much as she can throughout the week. It's a lot for Kenzie though and...her mom is...her mom's not doing well."

I close my eyes, letting out a sigh. Sitting in this fucking bed, not able to help Genevieve is killing me.

"A week? I've been out that long?"

"Mac, we're really lucky you even woke up at all. It wasn't good. You lost a lot of blood, your lung collapsed, and you went into shock and..."

She starts crying again and I squeeze her hand tighter.

"I'm fine now, okay? Why don't you get everyone else and the doctor so we can figure out when I can get the hell out of here."

She nods and stands, wiping her nose with the back of her hand.

"I've missed you, Val...so much. I love you."

"I love you, too. I've missed you all so much," she says, bending to kiss my forehead.

I lean my head back, thinking about my siblings and about what Valentina said. Running towards Jeremy, knowing I possibly was going to die scared the shit out of me. Not because I was afraid of dying, but because I was afraid of missing out on a life I could have had. A life with Genevieve and Kenzie. A life I'm going to have, no matter what obstacles Genevieve Langston puts in my way.

A soft knock on the door causes me to look up and immediately I smile. Despite the puffy eyes, the red rimmed pupils, the crazy hair and wrinkled clothes, she's beautiful...so fucking beautiful.

She starts to cry and rushes to my side and I lift my arm, cradling her head to my chest.

"I'm s-so sorry, Machlin. I'm so, so s-sorry. What I s-said to you, I--"

"Shhh. Stop, Genny. Don't apologize. We both said shitty things, it doesn't matter anymore, okay?" I say, lifting her chin to look at me.

She furrows her brows and I smile, wiping at her cheeks.

"I love you, Genevieve Langston. You bratty, little pain in my ass. I love the fucking shit out of you. I don't care how we started, I don't care about all the shit we slung at each other, I just love you. When Jeremy had that gun, I thought...I thought he hurt you and I lost it. Thinking about living a life without Kenzie and you scares me way more than taking a chance. I may fuck up, I probably am going to fuck up...a lot, but I know making up with you is going to be worth it. I've...I've never been in love, Genevieve. That woman I told you about, she just wanted my money and that wasn't love. This though, I've never felt this before and I didn't know how to do this, but now, I don't know how not to. I want you, Genevieve. I know we have our own shit to work on but that doesn't mean we can't help each other through it...as a team, not enemies."

She smiles through her tears and lets out a laugh as she wipes them away.

"I like your borderline sexual harassment remarks though," she whispers.

"And I like your sassy, fuck off comebacks. Can we do this? Date? Be serious? Be mine? I won't be able to stand it if you say no and I'll just have to black ball you throughout all of Arizona so no one will even think of dating you and you have no choice but to say yes."

She scoffs and runs her thumb down my lip, silently nodding with that sexy little smirk.

"You're an arrogant bastard, you know that?" she whispers.

"Your arrogant bastard?" I ask with hope.

"Okay," she says softly. "Mine."

Chapter 25
Machlin

Three months later...

"Are you sure about this?" Genevieve asks nervously. "I mean...you don't even know her, Machlin. She's half me. What if you hate her? What if she relapses at the house? I'll never forgive myself for bringing her here and--"

I cut off her rant with a kiss, slipping my hand around her waist and pulling her flush against me. Her hand slips around to the back of my neck as she pulls my head down, deepening the kiss. I smile against her lips, spinning us around and slamming her back against the car door, pressing my body into hers.

"Well if this isn't the most awkward reunion I've ever been a part of. You guys are real estate agents, no? Get a damn room."

Genevieve pushes off my chest and looks up, her eyes watering.

"Mama?"

"Hi baby," her mother says, giving her a smile as she drops her bag and opens her arms.

Genevieve runs to her as they wrap each other in an embrace and they both laugh through their tears.

"I've missed you so much. I'm so sorry for leaving and--"

"Don't apologize, my girl. I'm the parent, I'm just happy you didn't give up on me. Your father...he wouldn't have wanted me to live like that. I could never ever thank you enough for all that you did," she whispers, cupping Genevieve's cheek.

"Well I had help. Mama, this is my boyfriend, Machlin Saddler. Machlin, this is my mama, Leslie Langston."

I put my hand out for Leslie to shake and she pulls it, bringing me in for a hug.

"It's nice to meet you, son. Thank you for everything. I know the smile on my daughter's face probably has something to do with you, so thank you for that, too."

"It's nothing, really. I'm glad you'll be staying with us. You've raised one hell of a woman here, I must say."

Genevieve rolls her eyes and her mother slaps her hand.

"Don't be rude, honey. The man is paying you a compliment."

"Mama, you have much to learn. You're going to be looking for your own place by the end of the week living with us two," Genn laughs.

"Well if that greeting was any indication, I might," her mother says, raising her eyebrows.

"Oh Lord, I've missed you, Mama...so much."

Genevieve hugs her mother again and I watch as Leslie tears up.

"So many years you've had to fend for yourself. Never again, baby. Never again. I'm here and I'm not going anywhere."

I see her mother wipe her eyes and Genevieve wipes the other side, cupping her mother's face.

"I...see someone. Maybe you should come with me to a session. It might be good for us," Genevieve says softly.

"Oh honey, I'm so sorry."

"Don't be, Mama. It's not just for all that. It's for Tonya too, raising Kenzie...it's been a lot, but it's been good. I feel different...stronger."

"You've always been strong, Genny," I whisper, kissing the top of her head.

"Sparring with you will do that to me, *boss*," she says with a wink. "How about we head home and you really meet Kenzie this time? She's a little sweetie, you'll love her," Genn says, pulling her mom towards the car.

I grab Leslie's bag from the floor and put it in the trunk, driving us home.

Genevieve and Kenzie moved into my house a few weeks ago, hoping her mother will be well enough to live in her old house when she's ready. It's been an adjustment, but Kenzie hasn't had one nightmare since moving in.

We took her to the department store in the city and let her rack up my credit card with a brand-new room. The one thing Genevieve couldn't part with was her bed frame that her and her father built, and Kenzie loved it. Rochelle surprised her with a painting day, and they painted unicorns and mermaids on the sides, going with the theme of her room.

I glance over to Genevieve, watching her brows pull together as she looks at her phone.

"What's the matter?"

"It's Val. She uh...took a gig in Greece."

I sigh, knowing my sister wasn't going to last long in the states. After the shooting at the office she stayed at her house but quickly retreated to her cabin. A few weeks passed and she moved on to New Mexico, then somewhere in Colorado. I was waiting for the other shoe to drop and here it is.

"Well, she'll eventually have to come back for the wedding," I say.

"Wedding?" Genevieve gasps.

"Elijah and Gretchen," I say, with a smirk.

"Machlin Saddler, you bastard," she snaps, slapping my chest.

"Son, you let her talk to you like that? I swear, I didn't raise her to be such a sassy, little loudmouth," Leslie gasps.

"Mama, you did too!" Genevieve laughs, looking towards the back seat.

"I plead the fifth," Leslie smirks.

I laugh and shake my head.

"I think I might be the one looking for a place to stay. I don't know if I can handle *two* Langston women!"

We drive the rest of the way, making small talk. Genevieve and her mother catching up on different events over the years.

Rochelle and Kenzie are on the porch and Kenzie gets to her feet quickly, running towards us.

245

"LeeLee!" she yells, wrapping her arms around Leslie's legs.

Leslie drops to her knees and wraps Kenzie in a hug, silently sobbing into her hair.

"What a beautiful little girl you are," she says, pulling back to look at Kenzie. "What do you have going on over there?"

She nods towards the porch and we all follow an excited Kenzie.

"Hi Mrs. Langston, I'm Rochelle, Machlin's sister. Great to meet you," Rochelle says, extending her hand.

Leslie pulls my sister's hand to give her a big hug and Rochelle laughs.

"You Saddlers are lookers! My grandbabies will be little models."

Genevieve coughs from behind us and I turn, smirking at her.

"Oh, they will be."

She gives me that death look and I laugh, turning back towards Kenzie.

"Baby bed!"

Kenzie holds up the mini crib her, Genn and I have been working on for her baby doll.

"You got LeeLee excited! Maybe your ma--" Leslie stops and looks over at the two of us.

"What...does she call the two of you?" she asks.

Genevieve shrugs.

"She sometimes calls me Mama but I don't push her to. She still calls Machlin, Man," Genn laughs.

Leslie laughs too, turning towards Kenzie.

"Maybe your mama and man will let you help them build a real one when you get a little sister or brother."

"Mama!" Genevieve gasps. "Stop! We aren't even married."

"Not yet," she winks. "Now I heard you're a phenomenal cook, Rochelle. Rehab food could have been the death of me."

"Yes ma'am," Rochelle laughs, lacing her arm through Leslie's as they walk inside.

Kenzie pulls on my shirt and I look down.

"Man. Baby need chair," she says.

"Okay, cutie. Let's go get some stuff for a chair."

I lift her up on my shoulders as we walk through the house towards the backyard and the garage.

I put Kenzie to her feet and start looking for materials.

"Thin wood sticks, like this," I tell Kenzie making the motion with my hand.

She nods, looking through all the small wood we have in the corner.

I grab the wood glue and a few pieces for the back of the chair and the seat and feel a hand on my back.

"Sorry about what she said. She's not being serious, I don't want you to feel pressured," Genevieve whispers from behind me, kissing my neck.

"It didn't bother me. I do plan to make a crib for our baby, when we have one," I say with a smile, turning to face her.

"We definitely will. All three of us."

"Kisses?" Kenzie says, from between us.

Genevieve and I laugh as we kiss each other and then lift her in between us, smashing her cheeks with a kiss.

She laughs and my chest pulls with love. *Almost, Machlin. Almost.*

"I'm about to give Kenzie a bath and get her ready for bed. You good, Mama? Need anything?" Genevieve asks.

"I'm good, baby. I'll see you in the morning."

Genevieve kisses her cheek and gives her a hug, giving her the genuine smile that I grew to love so much.

"I'll be waiting up for you in bed, *boss*," Genevieve says with a wink.

I kiss her softly on the lips, then Kenzie as I watch them both climb the stairs.

"So..." Leslie says, eyeing me, crossing her arms over her chest. "You gonna try to make a decent woman out of that one? I know it's damn near impossible, but you seem like a man that can get pretty close. I wasn't kidding before."

I laugh, realizing how similar Genevieve is to her mother. The sass, the no bullshit attitude, the honesty. I can see a change in Genevieve, having her mother here and I love it.

It's good for her, a suggestion by her therapist that couldn't have been more accurate. I knew I had to do something when she confided in me that while I was in the hospital, her mother was on another floor getting her stomach pumped, breathing tubes, barely making it out alive.

"I was waiting for you to get better. I've had a ring for a while now. I want to marry her, and I want your permission," I say, letting out a breath.

"Well you got it," she says, getting up from her chair.

"That's it? You barely know me."

"I know that any man that can handle a Langston woman, deserves her. The second you opened your mouth you reminded me so much of my husband. That man drove me up a damn wall, but you know what? I did the same," she says with a laugh. "He...was a great man, a *passionate* man and he gave me a love I would never forget. Take care of her, Machlin. I won't be around forever and she's going to need you to keep that smile on her face. If you can do that, you can marry her."

She slaps me on the back, and I stand, pulling her in for a hug.

"Thank you, Mrs. Langston. I promise I will."

"Call me Leslie, Machlin. We're family now."

I nod as she walks down the hallway to the guest room and I run upstairs, checking on Kenzie. She's fast asleep so I make my way down the hall, opening our bedroom door and smile. Genevieve's passed out on top of our comforter in one of my t-shirts, the bottom of her ass cheeks peeking out from the hem.

I walk around to my nightstand, opening the top drawer and reach behind my underwear. I wanted this to be special...extravagant, but I'm too fucking excited to wait. I kneel down on her side of the bed, the ring box open in my hands and flick my finger against her ass. She slowly opens her eyes and groans.

"Let me sleep."

"Wake up, you brat. I have something I want to ask you," I laugh, flicking her ass again.

"Unless it's, 'do you want to sit on my face', then ask me in the morning," she says yawning, rolling over into my hands.

She jumps when she realizes what she bumped into and bolts up in bed

"M-Machlin what...what is that? Why are you kneeling?"

"Genevieve Langston..."

"Oh my God."

"You have turned my world upside-fucking-down and I never want to turn it back up. You crashed into my life and it has never been the same. I asked you on the first day we met if you believed in fate and at the time, I wasn't sure I did, but I do now. I never told you this but on the way to the airport in Spain, my car broke down and we had a flat tire, missing my original flight. It was fate that I got on that other flight that day, meeting you, working alongside you, falling in love with you. You will always be a pain in my damn ass, but you are *mine* and I am *never* letting you go. Will you be the CFO of Saddler Enterprises?" I ask with a smile.

She smiles too but then it falls when my words register.

"The...CFO? I...I thought..."

"And...my wife?"

I open the ring box and she laughs, slapping my chest as she wipes a tear.

"Machlin Saddler, you son-of-a-bitch! I almost just cried, you asshole! This doesn't have anything to do with what my mama sa--"

"No," I say, cutting her off. "I've had the ring burning a hole in my underwear drawer, waiting for her to get better so I can ask."

"You amaze me, you know that?" she whispers, cupping my cheek. "Of course I'll be your wife but are you sure about the CFO? I'm still so new and--"

I cut her off with my lips, slipping the ring on her finger then break the kiss.

"I'm sure. Elijah and I talked about it and you were the one for the job all along."

"Going to rule the real estate world together, huh, King Saddler?"

"A king is not a king without a queen. You are my queen, Genevieve Langston."

I run my thumb down her bottom lip and she winks at me, biting the tip.

"Don't forget it, *boss.*"

Three months later...

I walk into Machlin's office and see him standing in front of his window, arms crossed. I stride over to him, running my hand down the back of his crisp suit jacket.

"Stress will give you wrinkles, old man," I whisper, kissing the back of his neck.

"Good thing I know a woman who knows how to distress me then," he smirks.

He turns, giving me a big smile and kisses me, spinning me so my back is against the glass of the window.

"I can't wait to fucking marry you," he growls, kissing down my neck.

"Mmmm, me either," I moan, gripping his arms.

"Are you sure I can't fuck you against this window?"

"As...tempting as that is, I want to wait until tomorrow," I whimper, feeling his hands slip between my legs.

"What about this?" he asks. "Can I make you come like this?"

His fingers slip inside my thong and brush against my wet folds.

"Mac, the door is--"

"Jesus Christ, come on! Shut the fucking door!" Rochelle snaps, reaching for the handle and slamming Machlin's door shut.

I laugh and smack his hand away, righting my thong.

"Tomorrow! Stop making me break my rules. You have a habit of doing that," I smirk.

"It's been a week, Genny. A fucking week! I'm dying, can't you see it? I'm pale, my hair is greying. You saw the wrinkles and you said so yourself!" he says dramatically, pulling an arm around my waist to sit on his lap in his desk chair.

"Oh, stop it! I just want the next time you're in me to be as my husband."

I kiss his lips softly then pull back.

"Why are you stressing and don't say lack of pussy," I say, pointing at him.

He lets out a sigh and shakes his head.

"Val...is going to lose her shit tomorrow."

"Did Elijah say why he invited Declan? I'm a little pissed because it wasn't his place. If he wanted to invite him, he should wait until his wedding. This is *our* day and I don't want one of my bridesmaids upset."

"Elijah is the only one that knows what went on between the two of them, so I guess he knows what he's doing. I just...want to fucking kill Declan. I mean he was my best friend...Val isn't the same since they split and I..."

"Cannot fight him at our wedding. Promise me, Machlin, you won't cause a scene," I say, putting my pinky out towards him.

"Okay, okay, I won't cause a scene, unlesssssss he does something to Val. If he makes her cry or puts his hands on her--"

"Valentina can hold her own. I thought we were loosening the reins a little," I say, arching an eyebrow.

"Yes, yes, fine," he groans.

"God, you're so grumpy when you haven't eaten!"

"You're right, I am a little *hangry*. Luckily, my favorite meal is right here," he says, spreading my legs.

I laugh and slap his hands, getting to my feet. "Tomorrow...in my wedding dress, wherever you damn well please, *boss*."

I wink and walk out of his office, heading home to get ready for our rehearsal dinner.

"When I said...in my wedding dress...I meant--"

"Fuck, what you meant," Machlin snaps, lifting me up and slamming my back to the door of the bridal suite. "You said wherever I want, and I want you right fucking now, *wife*."

He pushes my thong to the side and slams into me, latching onto my neck with hungry kisses.

"God, say it again," I pant.

"My *wife*," he growls against my lips.

I moan against his mouth as he pushes harder into me, his shaft rubbing deliciously over my clit, already bringing me to the brink. One week is too long. My body stretches for him as he continues his grinding, planting his feet firmly on the floor and pounding my body into the door.

"God, I'm so close. So, so close," I whine.

"You guys are the worst!" we hear an angry whisper say from the other side of the door. "Everyone is waiting to see you!"

Dakota.

I smirk and lick up the side of Machlin's neck like a lollipop as he squeezes my thigh, digging his fingers in.

"It's *cock*tail hour, Dakota," he says with a laugh.

"Jesus, what are you five? It's not funny, hurry up!"

We stare at each other, listening as we hear footsteps echo back down the hallway.

We both laugh as Machlin lifts me, carrying us to the couch and he sits, as I straddle his lap.

"You want me to be on top, *husband*?"

"That's how you do your best work, isn't that right, Mrs. Saddler?"

"God, hearing you say that turns me on," I groan, starting my rhythm on top of him. "And you didn't shave. Am I finally going to be able to ride your mustache?"

"All night, *wife*. You can ride it all fucking night."

I moan, gripping his shoulders and bounce higher, slamming back down on him. The familiar feeling of rapture courses through me and knowing it's because of love--not because I'm trying to escape something--relaxes me. I slam my lips to his, letting go of the tension in my lower belly and my body squeezes him as I feel him explode inside me with a groan.

"I love you," I pant against his mouth.

"I love you too, Genny."

We walk into the cocktail hour a few minutes later and my face heats as everyone cheers, wolf whistling and cat calling.

"Officially consummated!" Rochelle yells, tipping her glass up.

Everyone laughs and I shake my head, flipping her the middle finger.

"Fuck off," I mouth to her.

"I might," she mouths back, nodding to the guy standing next to her.

I laugh and roll my eyes as Machlin walks me around, saying hello to all our guests.

I'm lost in a conversation between Machlin and one of our clients when I see a man standing at the bar, tossing back drinks by himself. His dark blonde hair is styled in a sad attempt at taming it. When he turns, I can see his scruffy beard and gorgeous, dark blue eyes...like Chris Hemsworth. Good Lord.

"Who is that?" I ask, pulling on Machlin's jacket.

I watch as the man turns towards the other side of the bar where Valentina is doing the same. Tossing back drinks like a 300 pound man.

"Oh Jesus. That's...that's *the* Declan?" I whisper.

I watch as he stares at Valentina and she starts to take out her clips, one by one until her long, brown hair falls down her back. She's so gorgeous and remembering her saying she used to be blonde pops into my head. I still don't know why she dyed it, only that it was after her and Declan split.

He looks miserable, they both do. If they're both so sad, why the hell did they break up in the first place?

I quickly register a large man in a suit walking towards Declan and realize it's Machlin.

"Shit!" I whisper, following behind him quickly.

I hear his angry voice as he says something to Declan I can't make out.

"Don't plan on it, believe me. Ship has sailed and sunk, not reviving it," Declan says back.

I put my hand on Machlin's back and come up next to him. "We're behaving, right *husband*?"

"Always beautiful. Just making sure my old buddy here doesn't try and fuck my sister again."

"Just fuck, huh?" says a voice from behind us.

I turn and Valentina is there, a smirk on her face.

"More like marry, right *ex-husband*?" she slurs.

I smell the whiskey coming off her and I feel Machlin's back stiffen against my hand. My jaw drops at her confession.

"Ex-husband?" Machlin growls.

"Whoops," Valentina says with a giggle

She slaps Declan's chest as she walks away with a laugh and Declan tries to turn to go after her. Machlin stops him, slamming his hand to his chest.

"Tell me she's drunk off her ass and messing with me, Declan!"

"Not now, Mac. Kick my ass later, I need to have this out with your sister."

He brushes past him and Machlin, exhales, running his hand down the front of his face.

"Let it be, Mac, it's our wedding."

"Did you know they were married?" he asks.

I shake my head. "I don't even think Rochelle knows. She never refers to him as Val's ex-husband."

"God, why would she choose to tell me this now?" he groans.

"Because she's drunk and hurt and he's really hot. It would be a lot easier to hate him if he wasn't so damn hot. I mean doesn't he look like--"

I stop my words when I see Machlin's jaw twitching and give him a sheepish smile.

"I love you."

He rolls his eyes and grabs my ass, roughly pulling me towards him.

"Oh, my wife. You've much to learn. You'll pay for that one."

I'm sitting at Val's kitchen island, cutting peppers for our family dinner. She wanted to get everyone together for a big family meal before she heads back out of town.

After seeing Declan at our wedding last night, I figured she would already be gone, but holding this dinner tonight makes me think we won't be seeing her for a long time.

The bomb of their marriage threw everyone for a loop, and she refuses to talk to anyone about it. I volunteered to come early and help her cook, see if she wanted to talk to someone other than her siblings, but it's been silent; the only sound is the knife on the cutting board.

The doorbell rings and I glance at Val.

"Want me to get it?"

"Would you?" she asks, distractedly.

I nod and walk towards the front door, looking through the glass window up top.

No one.

I open the door slowly and look down and come face to face with a little girl maybe around ten. Her hair is a mop of dirty blonde and she has the lightest blue eyes I've ever seen. The only other people I've seen with that shade are Elijah and...

"Is Valentina Saddler here?" asks the little girl.

Her voice is strong and confident, the opposite of what I pictured when she opened her mouth.

"I...yeah, who's asking?" I respond confused.

"I...I'm Faith."

I nod and look down at her, still confused.

"Okay Faith. Is she um...expecting you?"

"No I...I'm...I..."

"Who is it, Gen?" Valentina asks from behind me.

I glance over my shoulder and look at Val and she drops her phone out of her hand, sending it crashing to the wood floor. Her jaw drops, her eyes water, the same blue eyes that...

I look back to the girl and she too has her mouth agape, staring at Val.

"My God," Val gasps.

"I...I'm your daughter," the girl whispers.

I look back between the two, just standing there until the dam breaks and Valentina rushes forward, scooping the girl into a hug.

"I didn't think I would ever get to hold you again," Valentina cries.

"I...I wasn't...I'm sorry I'm here but...I have...no one," sobs the girl.

"Shhh, it's okay," Valentina soothes. "It's okay."

They both cry, holding each other tight as if they would float away if they let go. I watch, my mouth open and tears streaming down my own face. I had no idea Valentina had a baby. How had Machlin never told me before?

"No one knew except Elijah," she whispers, as if she can read my mind. "I was young and...sweetie what happened?" Valentina asks, breaking the hug and pushing the little girls chin up to look at her. "I thought you would be okay. I got pictures every year and they told me you were okay."

"I was b-but...I..."

She starts to cry again and Valentina hugs her again.

"Come and eat something, then we'll start at the beginning, okay?" Valentina consoles.

"Yes, someone please start at the beginning," I agree.

Valentina looks up at me, grabbing the girl's hand and nods towards the kitchen.

"We need wine," she says. "Lots of wine."

Thank you so much for reading the first book in my new series! I hope you enjoyed it and if you did, let me know by leaving a review or getting in touch with me!

Stay tuned for Valentina Saddler and Declan O'Sullivan's story next! Their prequel...Saddler's Start will be released on October 15th and their full length novel will be released November 11th! Pre-orders for Saddler's Sacrifice are being donated to The Fischer House Foundation! For more info, visit my reader's group Nicole's Naughty Nook !

Saddler's Start
Saddler's Sacrifice

Make sure to follow me on social media for new release updates, giveaways, sales, etc!

Bookbub: https://www.bookbub.com/profile/nicole-rodrigues

Goodreads: https://www.goodreads.com/author/show/18587431.Nicole_Rodrigues

Twitter: https://twitter.com/nicole_author

Facebook: https://www.facebook.com/nicolerodriguesauthor/

Instagram: https://www.instagram.com/nicolerodriguesauthor/

Other books by Nicole Rodrigues:

The Double Play Series
Curveball
Going, Going, Goner
Ballers With Benefits
Changeup
Walk Off
Last Round

Layla & Hudson Duet:

Always in Your Corner
Pinky Promise

Made in the USA
Monee, IL
06 November 2020

46817399R00152